TENDERFOOT

Something moved behind Cochran and a strong arm crooked around his neck. He found himself held from the rear in a stranglehold. A voice, filtered through gritted teeth, spoke directly into his right ear.

"Why were you following me?"

Cochran tried to turn his head; the stranglehold tightened. "You know who I am, innkeeper!"

Cochran knew and his legs went weak, but only for a moment. With an almost random wrench of his body and gouge of his elbow, he pulled free of the arm that held him and pounded his assailant in the stomach. The man's breath burst out and he staggered back.

Cochran spun on his heel, straightened his glasses, and took on a boxing pose that would have brought forth a roaring laugh from Frogg, had he been there to see it.

His attacker didn't laugh; Cochran had actually hurt him.

SNOW SKY

Cameron Judd

BANTAM BOOKS

NEW YORK • TORONTO • LONDON • SYDNEY • AUCKLAND

SNOW SKY
A Bantam Book / November 1990

DOMAIN and the portrayal of a boxed "d" are trademarks of Bantam
Books, a division of Bantam Doubleday Dell Publishing Group, Inc.

ISBN 0-553-28800-8

Published simultaneously in the United States and Canada

Bantam Books are published by Bantam Books, a division of Bantam
Doubleday Dell Publishing Group, Inc. Its trademark, consisting of the
words "Bantam Books" and the portrayal of a rooster, is Registered in U.S.
Patent and Trademark Office and in other countries. Marca Registrada.
Bantam Books, 666 Fifth Avenue, New York, New York 10103.

PRINTED IN THE UNITED STATES OF AMERICA

OPM   10 9 8 7 6 5 4 3 2

This book is dedicated with gratitude to Greg Tobin.

Chapter 1

For the third night in a row, the man forced the boy up the mountain trail. The higher they climbed, the louder pealed the thunder and the harder fell the rain, driving down in bullets and drenching them as they ascended. The man's hat had long ago soaked through and now sluiced water off its downturned brim and onto his wide shoulders.

Rain mixed with tears on the boy's face as the man roughly shoved him forward. "Go on, you," he said. The boy bit his lip and, as always, said nothing.

Narrower grew the trail. Finally the rain slackened, then all but stopped. Clouds drooping heavily from the gray sky formed a drizzling mist about the pair, and fog rose from the emptiness to their right, where the trail gave way to a sheer bluff. The boy's feet slid on the muddy path; twice he fell, and twice the man swore and pulled him up. They went on.

When the land disappeared before them and they finally stopped, they stood atop a high peak, looking down onto dark conifer treetops bending in the wind. Lightning flashed simultaneously with the man's wicked smile. He reached menacingly toward the cringing but still-silent boy. . . .

Florida Cochran woke up with a scream. Man, boy, and mountain melted into the smooth darkness of her bedroom wall.

Tudor Cochran, her husband, bolted up beside her. Florida turned her wide moon face with its watery blue eyes on him; the moonlight was so bright through the window tonight that he could read the silent sorrow in her eyes.

"Same dream?" he inquired softly.

She nodded sadly.

"Flory, what am I going to do about you and your crazy dreams?" he asked, and then wished he hadn't, for he knew already what she wanted him to do. So far he had refused.

Someone approached the closed bedroom door quickly but unevenly; bare feet slapped, scraped against the oiled slab floor on the other side of the door.

"Mr. and Mrs. Cochran! Are you all right in there?"

Cochran called back, "Fine, fine, Reverend Viola. Flory just had that dream again." The inquirer in the hallway was a preacher who had been lodging in the Cochran Inn for two nights now, lingering to let a bruised foot heal before he continued on to Snow Sky. Both nights Flory had dreamed the same dream and screamed herself awake, and the tall, solemn clergyman had limped down to the door on his sore foot to make sure everything was all right.

The preacher padded arrhythmically back to his room and Flory settled back into her feather pillow. For the next several minutes she sniffed and from time to time dabbed her eyes with the sheet, pretending to hide it so Cochran wouldn't notice while really making sure he did. Cochran listened for a while, then sighed and sat up on the bedside and reached down for his boots.

"It's a curse indeed for a grown man to have a bladder the size of a pea," he muttered. He pulled on his boots, fumbled around on the bedside lampstand for his spectacles, then walked out. An outhouse stood at the edge of the woods behind the inn, over near the stable where the horses and mules shifted about quietly in the moonlight. Cochran crossed the yard. It was a beautiful night blessed with a cool breeze that carried wonderful scents of earth and forest upon its shoulders.

As Cochran walked back toward the inn, he stopped to gaze thoughtfully at the moon. After a few moments he looked at the ground, shook his head, and inwardly surrendered, pondering the sacrifices men have to make to keep their women happy. Over the years he had made several for Flory, and was about to obligate himself to her for one more. But he didn't much mind it, not really. Flory's happiness was worth it.

She was still awake when he returned. He slipped off his boots, tucked his nightshirt down about his knees, and slid back beneath the covers.

"All right, Flory, you needn't bring it up again. I'll go after them," he said.

She sat up, surprised. "You mean it?"

"If you think you and Theon can run things here without me for a while, I do."

"Of course we can. Oh, Tudor, you're a wonderful man."

His back was toward her, but he felt her smile beaming on him like sunshine through a window. It was good to know she was happy again, especially after all the worry her dreams had brought her. Cochran wondered why he had fought the inevitable as long as he had, plumped his pillow, and went back to sleep.

Breakfast was salt pork, eggs, and biscuits, the latter so hard that Cochran silently wondered if Flory had saved them from last Christmas. Flory had two main failings: she couldn't sing and she couldn't make biscuits, though she tried hard to do both, sometimes at the same time, which did not improve matters.

The Reverend P. D. Viola sat across the table from Cochran, shoveling big slabs of meat into his downturned mouth and gulping coffee from a china cup. Between bites he was talking about Flory's dream, in which he appeared interested even while also seeming preoccupied and somber. He had said a time or two that he had a dreadful duty awaiting him in Snow Sky, but Cochran was not a busybody and did not pursue the matter, nor had he allowed Flory to do so.

"There is sometimes a symbolism in dreams," the preacher was saying to Cochran. "Of what does this dream consist?"

Cochran described the dream based on Flory's slightly vague descriptions.

Viola said, "An image, perhaps, of Abraham taking his son up the mountain to sacrifice him."

"I don't think that's it," Cochran responded wearily, not enjoying the subject. "The boy and man in the dream were in here a few days back. Came late, stayed one night, and left early. The man acted edgy and the boy never said a word. He just looked at Flory a few times in a way that made her worry for him. She's had the dream three nights straight. She feels like the man is going to do bad to the boy. I don't know where she gets her notions."

The preacher bit off a piece of biscuit so hard it crunched like a bone. "Despite what you say, I find the imagery remarkably biblical," he said. "But even if not, perhaps her dream is meaningful in some other way. The story of Joseph and his interpretation of dreams gives us verification that sometimes dreams are a vehicle of insight from above and from within."

Cochran didn't really understand all that and was ready to drop it anyway. He took a swig of coffee and another bite of biscuit. A moment later Flory came in from the kitchen, smiling at Cochran more brightly than she had since their honeymoon nineteen years before.

"Anyone need more eggs?" she asked. She brushed past Cochran and patted his shoulder lovingly.

"A delicious meal, ma'am, and I'm satisfied," Viola said.

Cochran wondered how a preacher could voice such a lie; surely Viola had noticed the biscuits. Then again, maybe a grim fellow such as he enjoyed breaking his teeth. "A fine tableful to fit a man for a difficult encounter to come, and I'm about to go to one. My foot's in good enough condition, I believe, for me to travel on."

"My husband is to do some traveling, too," Flory

said, looking at Cochran and smiling again. "You'll be pleased. He's going off to do a good deed."

"Oh?" The clergyman looked inquiringly at Cochran. "Where are you going?"

"Snow Sky," Flory answered for her husband. Cochran wished she hadn't, for he knew at once what would follow: a suggestion from either Viola or Flory that the two men travel together. Cochran had nothing against Viola except his overly serious manner. Cochran himself was prone to be serious, but the preacher did not look like he had smiled since childhood.

"You plan to leave innkeeping for mining?" Viola asked.

"No. I'm just going on an errand for my wife. Nothing, really," Cochran responded.

"He's going to help a young boy in trouble," Flory said proudly, still beaming at her husband.

The clergyman raised his brows. "The boy in the dream?"

"Tudor told you about that? Yes, the very one. Now, Reverend Viola, I don't claim any gift of secret vision, but I just know in my heart that poor boy is in trouble. Tudor is going to find him and make sure he's safe."

"I see." The preacher turned to Cochran. "How do you know this man and boy are in Snow Sky?"

"Flory heard the man say something to the boy about Snow Sky. Besides, that's where everybody who travels this way is headed anymore."

"True. Speaking of travel, perhaps we could conduct ours together. I've been a bit melancholy, I admit, for I have already mentioned the unpleasant matter awaiting me in Snow Sky. A meeting with a person I dread encountering again. I could use a bit of good companionship on the road."

Cochran was glad he had seen that one coming. "I appreciate it, Reverend Viola, but I've already got a traveling partner." He shot a quick glance at Flory.

"Who?" Flory asked, surprised. She had thought he was going alone.

"Hiram Frogg," Cochran said.

Flory went dark as a snuffed candle. "If my husband intends to be in the company of Mr. Frogg, Reverend Viola, then you most assuredly do not want to travel with him," she said in a much cooler tone than before.

"Who is this Mr. Frogg?" Viola asked. "A strange name, Frogg."

"Just a friend of mine," Cochran responded.

"And a no-account of the worst sort," Flory added. "A common criminal. A thief and fighter—and he's been in jail."

"And got out again when his time was up," Cochran reminded his wife. "He's settled down a lot compared to what he used to be."

"He's settled, all right. Settled like an old hound too lazy to scratch his own fleas."

Flory had never liked Hiram Frogg, and had secretly hoped for a long time now that he would be lured away by the silver strikes at Snow Sky. So far, to her chagrin, he had not. Frogg was a most unambitious man, unattracted by anything that required labor. Frogg claimed to be a blacksmith, of all things, though he seldom actually worked. Flory suspected that her husband sometimes slipped Frogg money. He was soft like that, especially where Frogg was concerned.

Flory had never anticipated that Cochran was planning to take Frogg with him; she wondered if he had come up with the idea to get back at her for nagging him to make this trip. The fact was, Cochran actually hadn't considered taking Frogg until he realized a moment ago that he needed an out to avoid traveling with Viola. The more he considered it, though, the notion of taking Frogg along seemed good. Frogg wasn't much for brains or appearance, but he was comfortable to travel with, able to take care of himself. He would be a good companion in a swarming new mining town.

Viola stood, smacked lips smeared with grease and salt, then wiped his mouth on his napkin. "I must be off. I shall pray travel mercies for you and Mr. Frogg," he said to Cochran. "I trust you shall do the same for me. Perhaps we shall see each other in Snow Sky, or you'll catch up with me on the trail."

"Maybe so," Cochran said. "Preacher, that little Bible in your pocket's about to fall out."

"Indeed it is," Viola said, tucking back into his shirt pocket a thin, red-backed New Testament. "Mrs. Cochran, I'll gather my things and return to settle my bill."

When he was gone, Flory said, "I'd much rather you travel with a godly man than with a weasel like Toad Frogg."

Cochran bit off a piece of salt pork. "Don't call him Toad, Flory. You know that makes him mad."

———————————◆————————————

Hiram Frogg leaned over and spat a brown stream of tobacco juice onto the ground. He was sitting on his anvil, which, Cochran had noted, was dusty and strung with cobwebs from lack of use.

Frogg wiped a trace of brown juice from his lower lip and nodded. "I might go with you at that," he said. "Though it all sounds a little difficult. You think you can find a man and boy in that town? Snow Sky had nearly three thousand folks, last I heard, and more coming every day."

"The point isn't so much to find them as just to try, so Flory will be satisfied," Cochran answered. "You're right—it's a lot of trouble for little enough reason, but if you had a woman you loved you'd know why I'm doing it."

"What happens if you do find them?" Frogg asked, resetting his tobacco with his long tongue. That tongue, combined with his wide mouth, slightly bugged eyes, and unfortunate last name, were what had earned Frogg the nickname of Toad. But few dared call him that to his face, for he would fight anyone who did, friend or foe. His reputation as a brawler was one of many things Flory disliked about him.

Cochran shrugged. "I suppose I'll watch them and make sure the boy's all right. Maybe I'll talk to the man to see what his story is, if I think I need to. Mostly I just have to satisfy Flory the boy ain't been thrown off a cliff or something."

"Sounds crazy."

"No crazier than Flory will make me if I don't do it. She's thought of nothing else for days, and she won't let up about it. You see, Flory swears when that boy looked up at her while she was serving the table, she could see he was begging her for help. Begging with his eyes, Flory says, though he never said a word the whole time he was at the inn. Flory says something is wrong, that the man isn't the boy's father. And they didn't look at all alike, that's a fact."

"Do you know their names?"

"Not the boy's. Man signed in as John Jackson."

"Sounds made up," Frogg said.

"The world's full of John Jacksons. Besides, a man can make up a name if he wants. A lot of them do out here."

Frogg rose from his anvil and yawned. Some of the anvil's cobwebs clung to his dirty trousers. "Well, Tudor, I'll go with you, crazy and henpecked though you may be." He stretched. "I been wanting to get back to Snow Sky anyway, just to see how it's grown since the last time I was there."

Cochran was glad to see Frogg had at least some interest in Snow Sky. He had always thought that if Frogg could collect even half a basketload of ambition he might head to the mining town to set up a business. He could make a good living if he did. Blacksmiths were much in demand in mining towns, and indeed one of the first acts of Snow Sky's governing body, according to a copy of the Snow Sky *Argus* somebody had recently left at the Cochran Inn, was to put out an offer of a free building and house for any good blacksmith. Lawyers, saloon keepers, gamblers, and soiled doves Snow Sky had aplenty; skilled artisans it sorely lacked. Frogg wasn't a high-quality blacksmith, maybe, but he was honest and could beat out a decent horseshoe when he had to. Cochran had showed the story in the *Argus* to Frogg, but Frogg had not reacted.

Cochran himself had thought briefly of opening an inn or hotel in Snow Sky, but had decided against it. He had worked too long and hard establishing this one, and as long as Snow Sky kept attracting travelers, he figured he would thrive sufficiently right where he was. His inn's location about a day and a half from the mining town made it an almost essential stopover for westbound travelers to Snow Sky.

"When do we leave?" Frogg asked.

"Today. Get your things together, and I'll be back around in a little while."

"You're too good to that woman, Tudor. Running off on a fool's errand just because she squalls in the night."

Cochran adjusted his spectacles and said, "You just ain't been in love with anybody, Frogg. You don't love nothing but cards and sleeping late."

Frogg snorted. "I been in love plenty. Ain't met the first dance hall gal yet I didn't fall in love with."

Back at the inn, Viola was long gone and Flory was already packing Cochran's bag and bedroll. Theon, the skinny, slow-witted young man who helped the Cochrans run the inn, was sweeping out the main room. "Sure wish you'd take me to Snow Sky," he said to Cochran.

"You're needed here," Cochran answered. "You're too important to spare."

Theon smiled at the flattery and swept a little harder.

Seeing his bedroll depressed Cochran, who hated sleeping on the ground. He wondered if that was why he had become an innkeeper—to do his part to keep the human race from having to sleep outdoors any more than necessary.

"Don't you let Toad Frogg get you into trouble," Flory instructed sternly.

"I ain't a little boy, Flory."

"No, but Toad is. I really hate that you're taking him with you. You could have done better. That preacher Viola seemed a nice enough man."

"I'm sure he is. But he had too much starch about him. Frogg you can relax with."

"Oh, I'm sure. His idea of relaxing is gambling and drinking and I don't want to think what else. Don't let him tempt you to go to some cheap crib harlot, you hear?"

"I'm not in the market for crib harlots," Cochran said.

"What's a crib harlot?" Theon asked as he swept.

"Flory'll explain it when I'm gone," Cochran answered, grinning as Flory shot him a harsh look.

But a moment later she came to her husband and put her arms around him. Her gruffness vanished and she spoke tenderly. "Thank you," she said. "That little boy needs help. I know it as well as I know my own name. You'll help him if you find him, won't you?"

Cochran said, "If he needs it . . ."

He started to say more, but she planted a big kiss on his mouth and blocked off the words.

Chapter 2

The first night on the ground went as badly as Cochran had feared. He awakened stiff and aching, thoroughly repentant for his decision to make this trip and angry at Flory for having pushed him to it. Frogg, meanwhile, was as cheerful as ever. He had already built a fire and was frying bacon and corncakes in a spider skillet.

"Morning, Tudor!" he said. "Beautiful day for riding!"

Cochran rose and stretched, wincing. "I hope they got a good hotel in Snow Sky."

"Oh, they got plenty of hotels, but nothing as good as your inn. That's the trouble with a new mining town. You got to settle for what you can get, potluck all the way."

They ate breakfast silently. Three big cups of black coffee slowly brought Cochran back to life and washed the rust from his joints. By the time Frogg had rinsed out his skillet and poured off the dregs of the coffeepot, Cochran was in a much better humor, actually beginning to anticipate with some pleasure the visit to Snow Sky.

After all, a man had to see different scenes now and again just to keep from becoming stagnant. Cochran wondered if maybe he already was that way; he normally moved around about as much as a farm pond, and saw little more excitement. Maybe the trip would do him good.

As they rode, Frogg talked about Snow Sky, which had been founded beneath an overcast sky the previous year, 1889, on a snowy February day. An idle comment by one of its founders about snowy sky stretching above gave the town an informal name that finally had become permanent.

The silver chlorides at Snow Sky had assayed out at promising levels, and new, even richer lodes of silver and quartz were discovered by the week. Before the summer of '89 had ended, Snow Sky was a full-scale mining camp with twenty-five-cent beer and dollar-a-shot whiskey, flare-lighted streets, and scores of saloons, faro parlors, whorehouses, and lawyers' offices.

"You see if it ain't the next Leadville," Frogg said. "The railroad's already scouting out a route for itself."

"If you think so highly of Snow Sky, how come you don't live there?" Cochran asked.

"Been thinking about that. Maybe I'll stay on this time, open me a smithy."

Now that Frogg was actually talking about becoming a more respectable citizen, Cochran suddenly had his doubts. Frogg wouldn't be able to keep at his work with a lot of recreational diversions close at hand, and Snow Sky had plenty. Minimal law to supervise them all, too, although Cochran had read, in that same copy of the *Argus*, that the town's leaders had banded together to appoint a marshal and a small police force, and had built a jail.

The pair rode slowly but steadily almost half the day, not pushing the horses too hard, stopping twice to spell them. Cochran's mind had drifted away from the man and boy he was supposedly seeking, but when he and Frogg stopped about one o'clock for a meal he thought of them again, and wondered if perhaps Flory was right about the pair. She had good instincts, especially about children. Maybe she really had read a plea for help in the boy's eyes.

Then again, maybe it was just another case of Flory's feelings getting stirred up by the presence of a child. Cochran felt a pang. Flory's inability to give them children was a private wound they nursed together. Life was unfair; Flory would have made the finest of mothers.

They finished their beans and lay back beneath a tree to let them settle while the horses cropped the wild grasses. In a few moments Frogg was snoring with his hat pulled down over his eyes and his hands behind his head. Cochran, though, didn't nap; he got up after a few minutes and walked around, looking at the mountains with their evergreen slopes and barren expanses of stone made brilliant by the sunlight. A while later he went over and gently kicked Frogg awake, and they mounted up and continued.

They made better time than they anticipated, for it was not yet dark when they had ridden to within a half hour of Snow Sky.

The sunset was brilliant red and thick as maple syrup when Frogg stopped along the trail and dismounted.

He walked over to the trailside and picked up something from the ground. It was a small book of some sort.

"Let me see that," Cochran said, also dismounting. Frogg dusted the book off and handed it to him.

"This is the preacher Viola's little New Testament," Cochran said. "He almost dropped it from his pocket at the table yesterday morning. Must have lost it riding into town."

"Looks like a horse stepped on it," Frogg observed. "Pretty dirtied up."

"Yeah." Cochran wiped more dirt from it and started to put it into his pocket.

"Let me carry that," Frogg said, reaching for it.

"Why?"

"To bring me good luck."

Cochran handed the little volume to Frogg, frowning disapprovingly. "It doesn't seem fitting to use a preacher's lost Bible to bring you good luck in some faro parlor."

"Don't fret—I'll give it back to him, first time we see him. You just point him out."

They were remounting when Cochran suddenly stopped and walked over to the brush at the edge of the forest.

"What is it?" Frogg asked.

Cochran was peering down the wooded slope at the trail's edge. "Thought I saw something move down there on the ground," he said. "But I don't see anything now."

Cochran returned to his horse and mounted. As soon as he was in the saddle, he sniffed the air and made a face.

"What in blazes is that?"

Frogg grinned. "That, my friend, is the smell of a Colorado mining camp."

"Smells more like an open sewer from here."

"To you, maybe. To most folks hereabouts it smells like money."

———————————◆◆◆———————————

Thought it was not yet nine o'clock, already Earl Cobb had his hands full and was wondering why he could have been so foolish as to have accepted the job of Snow Sky town marshal. At the moment, as he slammed a hefty drunk against the saloon wall, pulling the man's knife-gripping hand around behind him and twisting it until the wrist almost snapped, he couldn't think of any good reason at all. He supposed he was a peace officer simply because that's all he had ever been, and all he knew.

The drunk roared and cursed as the knife clattered to the ground. Cobb kicked it away.

"Go at it, Marshal!" someone in the crowd hollered. "Whup that old boy real good!"

Keeping his grip on the painfully twisted wrist, Cobb leaned forward and put his face near the drunk's ear.

"You going to come quiet? Or do I break the wrist?"

"I'll kill you, Marshal, I swear it! Break your neck!"

Cobb twisted the wrist a bit more; the drunk screamed.

"I don't think you'll break anybody's neck with a busted wrist," Cobb said. "What I think you'll do is never threaten me again. You agree?"

With tears beginning to stream down his face, the man quickly nodded.

"Say it!" Cobb demanded with a shake and another scream-evoking twist.

"I won't hurt you, won't threaten you. Promise I won't!"

"Good. Now let's go sleep this thing off and get you human again."

He was grateful this Scofield Saloon and Gaming Parlor was close to the new town jail, which stood on the north side of the street officially named McHenry Avenue, but called Mud Street by everyone in town. Even Paul McHenry, the merchant-mayor for whom the street was named, called it Mud Street. Like most, he had taken a fall or two into the thick muck that made up the avenue after every rain.

Somebody opened the door of the Scofield and let Cobb and his prisoner out. Cobb steered the man rightward and down the crude boardwalk that ran in front of Kerrigan Brothers Hardware and Guns, then immediately right down Irish Alley toward the jail. Irish Alley, a narrow rut between buildings, was so dubbed because of its location between Kerrigan Brothers and O'Brien's Grocery. O'Brien lived in a relatively substantial house northwest of town out among an array of cabins and shacks, but the Kerrigans, two bachelor brothers, had built an apartment on the second level above their store. Right now Clive Kerrigan thrust his head out a window and called, "A good job, Cobb!" and pulled back inside.

"Thanks very much," Cobb muttered sardonically as he cut right out of Irish Alley into Jail Alley, which in turn led to the log-walled jail. Clive Kerrigan was on the town council and had been Cobb's chief promoter for this job.

Deputy Heck Carpenter stood up behind Cobb's desk as the marshal entered, slamming shut the dime novel he had been reading with much effort, limping from word to word like a drunk walking the ties of a railroad. "Why, hello, Earl. Didn't expect to see you so sudden."

"I can tell," Cobb said as he prodded his prisoner toward a cell.

"I won't cause no more trouble if you turn me loose," the drunk said.

Cobb shoved him into a cell. "I'll turn you loose after you sleep it off." He slammed and locked the cell door.

"Watch him, Heck. Don't let him hurt himself or nothing. I'll be back later."

He left the jail and walked back up the street, stretched, and scratched the back of his neck. Another long night ahead. Cobb had learned early on that he was needed mostly at night, and least in the mornings, so he worked the former and slept the latter. Sometimes he got no sleep at all.

He glanced to his right toward the intersection of Mud and Silver streets. In the intersection's center was the town well. At the intersection's southwest corner stood the Rose and Thorn Restaurant, the best eating establishment in town. One of the most substantial buildings, too; in Snow Sky many were more canvas than lumber, and good solid roofs of the sort on the Rose and Thorn were rarities.

The wind had been blowing from the mountains, northeast to southwest, carrying across town the smell of the Snow Sky livestock pens. A sudden momentary circling of the breeze brought a gust from the west to Cobb's nose, and he savored the aroma of food from the

Rose and Thorn's kitchen. His stomach grumbled hungrily. A good slab of pie and a cup of coffee was just what he needed to reward himself for hauling in one more drunk without getting stabbed or shot. Cobb had passed a firm rule against firearms in town, but lots of newcomers either didn't know about it or ignored it, and even those who carried no evident weapons often had hideout guns.

He strode to the restaurant and entered, sweeping off his hat and finger-combing his hair. Rose Tifton, who operated the restaurant with her husband, Kenneth (now, to his chagrin, increasingly being called Thorn because of the restaurant's arbitrarily chosen name), greeted Cobb warmly. Cobb liked coming here; the Tiftons were good people who wanted real law in Snow Sky. That was not a universally shared desire, particularly in the brothels, dance halls, and whiskey mills southeast of town.

"Come in, Earl. You're in luck—your table's clear."

"Why, thank you, Rose. You're a jewel."

"Good job with that drunk," Rose said as she seated him at his preferred spot, near the window. "I saw you taking him in. Ten policemen couldn't have done it better together than you did alone."

"I wish I did have ten policemen," he said. "Couldn't keep peace in a town like this when I had three men, and with Jimmy off with a broke leg I'm down to just two deputies. And Heck only counts for about half an officer. That drunk might be down at the jail hanging himself right now, and Heck would never know it. He keeps his nose stuck in cheap storybooks most of the time."

"It'd be no loss if that man hanged himself, I figure. I've got little patience for a drunk."

"Now, Rose. Half the population of Snow Sky are drunks. This one was just a newcomer a little too full of liquor. He might become a fine citizen when he's sober and digs himself into a good lode."

Cobb ordered vinegar pie, and Rose bustled back to the kitchen. For a moment there was no one else in the restaurant but Cobb. He savored the quiet, knowing it wouldn't last.

And it didn't. The front door opened and Jason Lybrand walked in. He looked straight at Cobb and came toward the table, his ever-present gold cross swinging from its chain around his neck. Cobb felt the same cool distrust for the clergyman that he always felt. Lybrand had been in Snow Sky for some time now, supposedly trying to turn his tent church into a real one, but so far, it seemed to Cobb, the preacher had been more interested in taking up collections than spending them on lumber and nails.

"Hello, Marshal," Lybrand said, seating himself uninvited. He seemed rather keyed up—not typical of him.

"Evening, Reverend. Got some coffee on the way if you want a bit."

"No, no thank you. Actually, I wanted to talk to you a moment. Sorry to do it while you're occupied."

"Don't worry about it. What's wrong?"

Lybrand looked even more worried. "Maybe nothing. It's just that there was a man scheduled to be here, at the latest, a day ago. He's another preacher, named P. D. Viola. He was planning to come here to help me try to stir a little more interest in building a proper church."

Cobb figured Lybrand had collected enough donations already for three proper churches, but kept the thought private. "And he hasn't arrived?" he said.

"He hasn't. And I've known Brother Viola for years. A punctual man. If he were delayed on the road away from a telegraph station, of course, there would be little way for him to contact me, and that's probably what happened . . . but still—"

Cobb's pie and coffee arrived; he smiled as Rose set it before him.

"Still, you're worried, right?"

"Right. I'm afraid some harm has come to him," Lybrand said.

Cobb bit into the vinegar pie. "Well, it isn't uncommon for folks to be delayed on those mountain roads. If he doesn't show up in a day or two we'll see if we can't find out where he is. Good enough?"

The preacher smiled tightly. "Yes, good enough. Thank you, Marshal. I feel better just knowing you are aware of the situation. I'll tell you if he doesn't show up tomorrow." Lybrand stood. "Good night."

" 'Night, preacher."

The clergyman walked out. A few moments later two more men entered the restaurant. The marshal quietly checked the newcomers over as he sipped his coffee; the action was instinctive and almost unconscious. Neither man struck him as an obviously worrisome sort, though the one with the wide mouth and scraggly whiskers did merit an extra glance. The other man looked particularly benign, like a schoolmaster. Maybe a banker or a preacher.

Preacher. Cobb wondered if this might be the missing P. D. Viola.

He finished his pie and coffee, left payment on the

table, and headed for the door. He paused at the table where the two men had seated themselves.

"Evening," he said, extending his hand. His friendly intrusion obviously took the two by surprise. "Earl Cobb, town marshal. Just wanted to welcome you to Snow Sky."

The mild-looking man shook Cobb's hand. "Tudor Cochran," he said. "Pleased to meet you, marshal."

The wide-mouthed fellow stood, scooting back his chair. He seemed a little nervous.

"Hiram Frogg," he said, also shaking Cobb's hand.

"Beg pardon?"

"Frogg. Hiram Frogg. Proud to meet you, sir."

"Same here." Cobb thought about asking if the pair had run across a preacher named P. D. Viola on the trail, but didn't, for he was having trouble squelching a laugh at the unexpected way Frogg's name fit his looks. Cobb didn't want to embarrass either himself or the other man, so he quickly turned away, saying, "I hope you enjoy your time in Snow Sky."

Thank you, Marshal. I appreciate your friendliness," Cochran said. He sounded weary, and looked like a man ready to find a bed and sink into it.

The marshal waved a goodbye to Rose and left the restaurant. Outside the wind was blowing in the same direction as before, carrying the stench of manure and livestock. Cobb put on his hat and sauntered down the Silver Street boardwalk, scanning the milling humanity in the flare-lighted street for anyone who looked like a troublemaker, a drunk, or a misplaced preacher.

Chapter 3

$\mathbf{C}$ochran and Frogg had left their horses with the old man at the public livery north of town before going to the restaurant. The livery was a big barn standing near the bank of Bledsoe Creek at the base of one of the mountains that overlooked the town. Scattered in an undesigned jumble all through and around town were scores of cabins and tents where the people of Snow Sky lived, most of them miners, a few with wives and families, the majority without. The mines themselves were farther northwest, in the rugged hills and mountain bases covered with evergreens.

True to Frogg's earlier statement, there was no good hotel or inn in Snow Sky, mostly rental rooms in various canvas-roofed log buildings around town. The pair had stopped at the first one they found. It was a long, narrow structure with a sign outside reading SCOFIELD RENTED ROOMS. It stood on Mud Street, next door to the Snow Sky Saloon and not far from the Blue Belle Dance Hall, which was little more than a big tent with rough wooden walls extending part of the way up. Music from an inept band carried through the thin walls and roof, unimproved by the filtering, and could be easily heard in the room Cochran and Frogg rented.

The music didn't much disturb Cochran, who was bone weary and eager for rest. After returning from the Rose and Thorn, he had immediately stripped to his long underwear and sank into one of the two sagging bunks in the room. In less than two minutes he was snoring.

Frogg was more restless, and the music did bother him. It made him think of cards, liquor, companionship, women. Frogg had more stamina than Cochran, and was not nearly as weary. After nearly an hour of staring at the underside of the canvas roof, he rose, quietly dressed, left the room, and walked onto the street.

It was only eleven o'clock; the saloons and dance halls would run full steam all night. Frogg grinned as he walked the gaudily lighted street up to the area of the town well. He looked up and down; as in most mining towns, there were abundant options for entertainment. Mining towns were inevitably filled to the bursting point with saloons and dance halls. The only enterprises they typically had more of were lawyers' offices.

Closest by Frogg was the Snow Sky Saloon, but he passed it up in favor of the Silver Striker farther down on Silver Street. This was one of the more substantial saloons and had a reputation for the coldest beer, thanks to the excellent ice house at its rear. Frogg got onto the boardwalk at the front of the Rose and Thorn and thumped down to his chosen place.

He walked into its warm yellow light and looked

around, hoping to see someone he knew. He had been to Snow Sky twice before. By his second visit the town had changed dramatically from when he first had come; he had already noted that the same held true this time. Snow Sky was growing, becoming more solid and permanent by the day despite the abundant tent structures and spit-and-wire wooden edifices still dominating the squatty skyline. All around town earlier tonight Frogg had seen the skeletons of new buildings that soon would replace their temporary predecessors. Lumber was stacked all about, ready to be hammered into new offices, businesses, homes, stables.

Frogg was disappointed not to spot a single familiar face in the tavern. But he didn't fret; if he couldn't find old friends he would simply make new ones. Right now a cold beer or two was the main thing he had in mind, anyway.

He went to the bar and got his drink, then followed it up with another. Another man also meandered to the bar. Within five minutes Frogg and he were talking; within ten they were seated at a table with several others, cutting cards for a poker game.

Frogg had little money to put up—he almost always had little money—but tonight fortune smiled. Little by little he gathered winnings, until at last his newfound friends were friends no more, and his broad-mouthed, toady grins were no longer quietly funny to them, but infuriating.

At last the man Frogg had met at the bar stood so quickly his chair tipped over behind him. He was very big and very drunk. "By damn, you look like a frog!" he bellowed. "I think you are a frog—and I'm going to feed you a fly."

Frogg's smile vanished. "I don't cotton to people funning with my name."

"What's the matter, frog? You about to up and hop off your lily pad?"

Frogg stood. "You talk civil or I'll feed you this chair."

The big man leaned across the table, palms flat. His face was six inches from Frogg's. "*Ribbit*," he said.

By now the other occupants of the saloon had turned their attention to the arguing men, and a general cheer arose when Frogg struck his antagonist in the mouth. This crowd favored a good fight anytime, for any reason.

The big drunk jolted back, and blood spilled from his split lip onto his chin. He dabbed it with his hand, examined it. "Get him!" he directed the others, all of whom were disgruntled with Frogg. "By damn, I will feed me a fly to that frog, I will!"

Frogg backed away, but others were on him at once. They found him hard to restrain, but the big drunk came forward and helped, and before long Frogg was pinned to the floor. The others in the saloon gathered around and looked down on him, grinning.

"He really does look like a frog—a big two-legged frog," a saloon girl said, then laughed.

"Here you go, Bill," somebody said. Frogg saw, to his dismay, a man hold out a wriggling something to the drunk above him. It turned and writhed between his fingers. "It ain't a fly, just a roach. Close as I could come."

"That'll be close enough," Frogg's antagonist said. "Get ready to eat your supper, frog."

Both Frogg and the doomed roach struggled for

freedom, neither successfully. Thick fingers pulled at Frogg's lips and tried to pry apart his clenched teeth. A finger slipped between his teeth and Frogg bit down, bringing forth a yowl as someone pulled back a bleeding digit. But that didn't stop the abuse. The liquored-up crowd was ready to see him devour the bug, and finally, despite all Frogg's efforts, someone managed to pry open his mouth. He closed his eyes as the roach fell onto his tongue. Before he could blow or push it out, his attackers forced his mouth closed. The bug crunched sickeningly between his teeth, and the crowd cheered and laughed.

The saloon owner was saying, "Here now—I don't want such as that in here!" Nobody listened.

Frogg wanted to spit out the crushed bug, but the men holding him would not let him open his mouth. Finally he swallowed it just to get it off his tongue. The crushed, crusty insect slid and scraped down the inside of his gullet.

"Feed him another one!" someone yelled. "Here—this is a big one!"

Frogg opened his eyes again. A much bigger roach wriggled above his face. Once again his mouth was being forced open—

He lunged, kicked, jerked, moved every way he could and found himself suddenly, unexpectedly free. Two of the men atop him had lost their balance and fell back. Frogg bounded up.

The big drunk who had launched the attack was stumbling backward, trying to steady himself. Frogg went straight for him with a loud yell. His fists swung out and connected. The man fell straight back.

Frogg dropped atop him, still pounding as hard as

he could. He felt flesh give beneath his fists, then warm red liquid was on his knuckles. There was now no laughter in the saloon; the people were hushed with panic. It was obvious to everyone that Frogg was mad enough to kill the man who had humiliated him.

For long moments the only noise was Frogg's fists making a dead thud against the face and neck of the supine man. Then the saloon owner yelled, "Get him off him!" and that was enough to break the freeze. Several men came forward at once and dragged Frogg off.

And then Earl Cobb was there, seemingly having appeared like a ghost. In fact, he had heard the noise from outside and walked in unnoticed just as Frogg had begun pounding the drunk. It had taken him until now to push his way through close enough to really see what was happening. Now that he did, he drew his Smith & Wesson Model No. 3 and fired into the floor.

"Hey, now—that's my property you're shooting!" the saloon owner protested futilely. In truth, the damage from the bullet made little difference, for the floor was made of heavy puncheons, and this was not the first bullet those thick split logs had absorbed.

"This ruckus is over," Cobb declared. "I want to know who started it."

Frogg would have spoken up, but his tongue felt like it was wrapped in cotton and his throat burned. He feared that bug he had eaten might make a reappearance.

Others spoke quickly: It was Frogg who started it, they said. Frogg just launched into Old Bill for no reason, just started pounding him in the face like he wanted to kill him, just because Bill had said Frogg looked like his name.

Cobb doubted what he heard, with Frogg being a newcomer. Bill was one of the more popular figures in Snow Sky's lower society. He figured Bill was being protected. But it hardly mattered. He had witnessed Frogg pounding Bill in the face, and that was what he had to respond to.

Cobb took Frogg by the collar. "Come on," he said. "You're going with me."

Frogg found his tongue buried somewhere in that cotton in his mouth. "I didn't do anything but defend myself," he said. "They put a bug down me."

A murmur of chuckles ran through the crowd. Cobb looked sharply around. "That true?"

"He's lying," Bill said, sitting up with his face covered with blood. "He jumped me for no cause."

Cobb suddenly was weary of it all. He pulled Frogg after him out the door, almost dragging him down the street.

"Where you taking me?" Frogg asked.

"The jail. You can spend the night there and think over trying to improve the way you get along with folks in this town."

"I didn't start it. They lit in on me."

"I don't doubt it, but I don't much care, either. Whatever your reason, I saw you just about kill a man, and I can't overlook that."

Frogg thought of Cochran, asleep back there in that rented room. Cochran didn't even know he had left. He started to ask the marshal if he could stop by the room long enough to tell Cochran what had happened, but realized the officer was in no mood to make an extra stop.

"They really did feed me a bug," Frogg said when

they reached the jail. The marshal all but shoved him in. He fumbled with the lock on one of the three iron-barred cells.

"Well, Frogg, there's plenty of bugs in there, if that first one gave you a taste for them," Cobb said. "Clean out your pockets."

Frogg did not argue. He felt a mild despair, mostly because he knew Cochran would be angry with him for so quickly finding trouble. Obediently he emptied his pockets and handed his possessions—including a derringer—to the marshal.

Cobb raised the weapon. "It's against town ordinance to carry a firearm in the city," he said. "You just earned yourself a fine."

That reminded Frogg—all that money he had won was still sitting back there on the table in the Silver Striker Saloon. He corrected the thought: used to be on the table. By now it surely was in the pockets of whoever had first noticed it lying there.

Cobb looked at the small New Testament Frogg and Cochran had found on the road into Snow Sky. "Well, you surprise me," Cobb said. "You don't look to be the religious sort."

"It's a good luck charm," Frogg mumbled, turning away.

"Didn't work very well tonight, did it?"

"Nope." Frogg went to the bunk and laid down, his back toward the marshal.

Heck Carpenter walked in from the street, looking tired. With one of Cobb's three deputies laid up at home with a broken leg, Heck and Cap Corley, the remaining lawmen, had been working extra duty.

"Got you another one," Cobb said. "Watch him."

"What did he do?"

"Murdered a bug by ingestion, I hear." Cobb walked out, leaving Heck confused. Sometimes Cobb said mighty strange things.

Cochran awakened and rolled over. "Flory?" he said. He remembered then where he was and sat up, rubbing his eyes. A sharp pain stabbed through his back and he groaned. Sleeping on this bunk was hardly better than sleeping on the ground. Worse, really, for it was too soft and made his back sore.

He looked at Frogg's bunk. Empty. Frogg was out early for breakfast, maybe. Yet that seemed peculiar, for the Hiram Frogg he had always known would sleep until noon if given half an excuse.

Cochran got up and dressed. He combed his hair, looking in the little mirror hanging on a nail in the wall, then went out onto Mud Street. He was hungry, though the smell of raw sewage in a narrow ditch beside the little rooming house briefly took away his appetite. This was one of the stinkingest towns he had ever been in.

Also one of the busiest: wagons creaking, people meandering, commerce under way. The rough-cut festival atmosphere of the previous night had faded; replacing it even at this early hour was a sense of rush and enterprise. Cochran walked slowly along, looking over the town, alternating between wondering where Frogg was and wondering if a man could find a good breakfast in Snow Sky without having to draw blood paying for it.

He found breakfast, though not a good one, and paid a price that made his eyes water. He had an extra cup of coffee to make the meal seem more worth the cost and, as he sipped it, considered raising the cost of a night's lodging at his inn to two dollars, maybe more. Based on Snow Sky prices, he wasn't keeping up with the market. The canvas-roofed excuse for a room he had slept in last night cost him a dollar seventy-five. Even sleeping in one of Snow Sky's one-room so-called hotels, which were no more than a dozen bunks scooted together, set a lodger back a dollar fifty a night. Disgusting, the prices of things in mining camps.

Cochran left the restaurant and walked back out onto the street. He felt out of place and rather ridiculous. His agreement to come to Snow Sky to spy on a man and some boy simply to satisfy Flory's whim seemed merely a foolish nighttime condescension here in the morning sunlight. Flory was too pushy. And Frogg, unreliable. Already he had disappeared without even the courtesy to say where he was going.

Cochran walked about the town for lack of anything else to do. All around him rang the sounds of town growth. From several directions he heard the rasp of sawmills that struggled to keep up with the soaring lumber demand. Wagons creaked past, horses clopped along, mules pulled sleds laden with lumber and nail kegs. Quite a town, this place, growing like a miniature version of Leadville at the height of its own boom a decade back.

In the milling crowds it seemed hopeless to spot Frogg or the man and boy Cochran had come to follow. Perhaps the thing to do was to return to the room and hope Frogg showed up soon.

Cochran turned and suddenly stopped. There they were: the man and boy, walking together on the other side of the street. Neither seemed to notice Cochran, who stood stock-still. For some reason his heart began to hammer. The man and boy turned a corner, and Cochran followed across the muddy street.

The pair moved fast, weaving in and out of the crowd. At times Cochran lost sight of them, but always picked them up again. He was glad he had spotted them; now he could truthfully tell Flory he had found them and kept an eye on them. He was pleased to see the boy did not act frightened of the man now; he marched along beside him readily.

They stepped into a boot and shoe shop; Cochran went to the bench outside the door, picked up a copy of the *Argus* that lay on it, and pretended to read. He heard the man inside, inquiring about shoes for the boy. Several minutes passed, then the pair came out again, the boy looking down at his two shining new pieces of footwear. Cochran lifted the paper to hide his profile and let them pass.

Cochran stood and followed them at some distance. All at once the man turned so unexpectedly that Cochran did not have time to react, and for a moment his eyes and the man's met and locked. Cochran broke the gaze and ducked quickly into an alley, wondering if the man had recognized him from the inn. A few moments later he ventured out again. The man and boy were gone.

In an isolated miner's cabin two miles from Snow Sky, a big man with dough-soft hands peered out through the eyeholes of a flour sack mask and pressed a knife to the throat of another man pinned below him. His victim was much smaller than he, though far more muscled and callused, for he was a miner and worked hard. The man with the knife pursued the less strenuous profession of robbery.

"I'll ask you one more time—where's your valuables?" the robber asked in a voice incongruously soft and high-pitched for a man his size.

The man pinned on the floor glared bravely back up at his attacker and said nothing. The blade pressed into the soft flesh beneath his chin.

"For God's sake, Orv—tell him! He'll kill you!" The woman who had shouted the words struggled to free herself from the grasp of a second masked man, who was armed with an old Colt pistol that he alternately waved toward the man on the floor and thrust against the side of the woman.

Wide-eyed and scared in the corner cowered a little girl of about two, watching.

"I'll tell you nothing!" the victimized man said, confirming his wife's frequent observation that he had more stubbornness, and less common sense, than most mules.

Kimmie Brown sent up a despairing wail. The robber with the knife nicked Orv Brown's neck a little, drawing blood.

"Still uncooperative, huh?" he said in his too-soft, too-high voice. "Think I won't really gape your throat, do you?"

"I won't give up what's rightfully mine to the likes of you," Brown said.

"Your life is rightfully yours. You willing to give that up?" The robber punctuated the query by scribing out another thin cut on Brown's neck. The line was pale for half a second, then turned red as it released blood.

"Orv, they'll kill us all!" the woman pleaded through tears.

Attention shifted to her. "Maybe you know where it is, pretty lady!" the man with the gun said, shaking her. "Talk up good unless you and the runt want to see your man smiling with his throat instead of his mouth." He laughed at his own crude attempt at wit.

"Don't say a word, Kimmie!" Brown said, his voice more tremulous now that he had taken a couple of cuts.

Kimmie ignored her husband. "It's under the floor—pull that board there." She pointed.

The robbers smiled beneath the masks. The one pinning Orv Brown moved off him. Brown, whose chest had been pressed under the robber's weight, took a deep, welcome breath and sat up.

"I should have figured that a shack like this wouldn't have a floor without some reason," the high-voiced robber said. "Get up and pull that board," he ordered Brown.

"You shouldn't have told, Kimmie," Brown muttered. He rose and walked across the little cabin to a corner. There he knelt and pressed one end of a floorboard. The other end seesawed up an inch; he got a grip on it and lifted it out.

The bigger robber came up behind Brown, grabbed him by the collar, and pulled him back onto his rump. "Up and over t'other side," he ordered. Brown, looking very sullen, obeyed.

The robber reached into the hole and pulled out a metal box. Popping it open, he nodded as he studied the mix of cash, silver, gold, and jewelry inside.

"The necklace was my mother's," the woman said. "She gave it to me on her deathbed. Won't you let me keep at least that?"

"Why, you're pretty as a picture without it, and your ma surely don't need no necklace no more," he said. "Get over here with your husband."

The woman, trembling, went to her husband's side. The child in the corner began to whimper.

"I'll hunt you down," Brown said to the robbers. "I'll find you and see that you pay dear for this."

"Shut up and turn around."

The woman put her hands over her face and obeyed, but Orv Brown stared defiantly, his chin thrust out, little trails of blood still running down his neck from the slashes the robber had inflicted.

The big robber shrugged. "However you want it," he said. He swung up his pistol and brought it down hard on Brown's skull. Brown shuddered and fell. The woman screamed and the little girl began crying in earnest.

The pistol went up, down again, and Kimmie Brown fell atop her husband.

"That ought to keep them from raising any ruckus for a while."

"What about the kid?"

"Leave her be. She can't do no harm. I ain't without conscience, you know."

The other man looked at the metal box.

"Sweet Mary, that's a pretty sight. But I know a certain partner of ours who'll be fit to be tied if he finds out about this."

"So we won't let him find out. Let's go."

The two robbers rode out onto the road that led into Snow Sky, their masks stashed in saddle pouches. The smaller man, Ivan Dade, halted his horse and pointed.

"Look yonder, Clure," he said.

Clure Daugherty did look, and saw a lone figure walking down the middle of the road toward them.

"He's alone. Let's wait and see what he's got on him," Daugherty said.

They waited, sitting mounted by the road. The figure kept coming, never slowing or speeding. He had one hand to his throat.

"My God," Dade whispered when the man was close enough to see clearly. "Let's get out of here."

Daugherty, who had gone pale, did not argue. The pair spurred and rode toward Snow Sky like they were being chased.

P. D. Viola stopped, lifted an imploring, blood-encrusted hand toward the departing riders, and tried to call out. He did not succeed, and they did not stop.

So he began walking again, staring straight ahead, clutching his throat.

Chapter 4

Viola walked into town, staring straight ahead with his hand still at his throat. The people of Snow Sky greeted him with stunned silence, for he was so bruised and swollen that he looked inhuman. At length a boy of about fourteen approached him as he might have approached a ghost and said, "Sir, do you need help?"

The only response was a faint, gruesome squeak from deep in Viola's throat. He fell to his knees, then collapsed. The boy's face went white. He turned and ran away.

A crowd silently gathered around Viola, who was prostrate and still.

"Is he dead?" someone whispered.

"I think so," another answered.

But Viola squeaked again and moved. "Get the marshal," somebody said.

Earl Cobb had just gotten out of his bed and pulled on his pants when the office door burst open and three excited boys ran inside. "Marshal!" they yelled. "Where are you, Marshal?"

"Here I am, boys," Cobb said, walking out from his curtained-off bedchamber as he buttoned his shirt. "What's the excitement?"

Three voices babbled together at top volume. Cobb waved his hands. "Whoa! One at a time! You—what's going on?"

The indicated boy stepped forward. "There's a man on the street, beat half to death. His throat's all mashed. He's big and tall, all bruised up. I think he's going to die."

Cobb nodded quickly. Without a word he returned to his bedchamber and pulled on his boots and hat. He strapped on his pistol as he walked out the door.

The boys ran ahead of him, leading him to the now-enlarged cluster of people gathered around Viola. Cobb pushed through and knelt beside the man, feeling his neck for a pulse. Viola squeaked again as if the mere touch of Cobb's fingers hurt.

"Get Walt Chambers," Cobb directed to any and all listening.

"I'm already here." A man broke out of the rim of the circle and knelt beside Cobb. Chambers was a self-taught horse doctor, and the closest thing to a real physician Snow Sky yet had to offer. The town fathers had been advertising in eastern newspapers for real doctors, but so far no one had taken the bait, and the town had to be satisfied with Chambers.

"He going to live?" Cobb asked after Chambers had rolled Viola over, rather too roughly, evoking a pitiful squeak. Chambers examined him cursorily.

"That I can't tell," he said. "Appears to me he's

been beat to within an inch of life. Let's get him to a bed somewhere."

"I've got a little cot off my office," said Herbert Hillyer, one of the town's myriad attorneys, whose office happened to be at hand.

"Thanks, Herbert," Cobb said. "Bring us a good wide board, somebody."

They scrounged a board from a nearby heap of lumber beside the shell of a new store, and on it carried the semiconscious Viola into Hillyer's office. Cobb shooed away the crowd and Chambers examined Viola more closely, breathing loudly through his nostrils in concentration. At last he straightened and shook his head.

"I'm amazed this man was able to walk into town," he said. "Truly astounded. He's about as busted up as old Pellenhymer was when we pulled him from the bottom of that mine shaft." The reference was to a fatality of a month before involving a drunk who wandered through a mining area after dark, looking for a missing dog, and fell to his death in an unmarked shaft.

"I wonder who he is?" Cobb asked.

Viola's eyes opened; the bloodshot orbs rolled about in their sockets, seeming at first unable to focus on anything, then finally picking out the faces of the men with him. The squeak came from his throat again, a terrible sound Cobb didn't like to hear.

"Your throat has been bruised very badly," Chambers said. "I don't think you'll be talking again for a long while." He smiled and touched the injured man's shoulder. "You just rest and let us look after you."

Cobb suddenly remembered the inquiry of Lybrand. He leaned close to the man on the bunk.

"Is your name P. D. Viola?" he asked.

The eyes widened; Viola squeaked again. Cobb understood.

"Who did this to you?" Cobb asked. Then he realized how futile it was to ask such a question of a man who could not talk.

But Viola seemed to want to answer. He moved his hands as if to indicate writing. Hillyer, who had been standing nearby, out of the way, went to his desk and brought back a pencil and paper. He handed it to Viola, but the man's swollen hands could not keep a grip on the pencil. Frustrated, the preacher squeaked some more, closed his eyes, and pressed his lips tightly together. Tears formed in the slits of his eyes.

"You can tell me later," Cobb said. "Right now the important thing is for you to—" He stopped, suddenly remembered the man he had jailed last night, the one who carried, of all things, a New Testament. Frogg— Hiram Frogg. That was his name.

"I got to go for a minute," Cobb said. "I got to check on something. I'll be back."

He went back to the office at a run and all but broke the latch going in through the door. He rushed to the desk and pulled open the drawer.

The red-backed New Testament was there. Cobb flipped it open, gave a mirthless smile, and nodded in fulfilled expectation.

On the inside cover was the inked-in name of P. D. Viola.

Lybrand was in his cabin with the curtain drawn across the window when Deputy Heck Carpenter knocked. The preacher scurried to put away the whiskey bottle and glass on the table, and gestured with finger over lips for the woman with him to be quiet. Straightening his clothing, he went to the door.

The deputy noticed the preacher's disheveled look. "You been sleeping late, Rev?" he asked.

"I haven't felt well," Lybrand answered. "I've been worried about a friend who has not yet arrived in town."

"If you're talking about that Viola, then I got some word for you from Earl Cobb: He walked into town this morning."

Lybrand looked surprised—maybe more than surprised. "What?"

"I said he walked into town this morning. But—sorry to tell you this—he's in a real bad way. Somebody beat him nearly to death on the road outside town, and he may die yet."

Lybrand seemed stunned. He stood silently for a couple of moments, seemingly trying to absorb the news. Suddenly his eyes flashed, and he asked, "Has he said anything... about what happened to him?"

"He can't talk. Looks to me like somebody tried to crush his neck. But don't you worry—we already got the one who did it over in the jail. A fellow name of Frogg who got into a ruckus in one of the saloons. Cobb found the preacher's little Bible in Frogg's pocket."

Lybrand stared blankly. "You've got the one... oh. Where is Brother Viola now?"

"In a little room off the side of the lawyer Hillyer's office. You know, preacher, this here town needs a hospital. Maybe you ought to lead a campaign to raise money for one, once you get your churchhouse built."

"Yes. Right. I want to see Viola—is that possible?"

"Course it is. But you'd best hurry, because I think he's going to die." Carpenter realized he was talking too frankly under the circumstances. "I'm sorry to talk so blunt. I shouldn't be guessing about stuff like that. I ain't no doctor—maybe he'll live after all."

"That is my prayer," Lybrand said. "I'm glad you have his attacker. Interesting that a copy of the very word of God would be the evidence of his guilt."

"Yeah. Good day to you, Rev. Got to go now."

"God bless you, my friend."

Carpenter walked away and Lybrand closed the door and leaned against it, still looking quite stunned.

Polly Coots, for reasons long forgotten called Dutch Polly among the ranks of Snow Sky's army of prostitutes, came to him from the corner.

"You talk awful pretty, you know it?" she said. "Almost as pretty as you look. I like that preachery voice. What was that deputy talking about?"

Lybrand was so deep in thought it took him a few seconds to realize she had spoken. "What did you say?"

"What was that deputy talking about?"

Lybrand shook his head. "Nothing to concern you. Just a problem I thought I had sufficiently dealt with—though it appears I was wrong. At least he hasn't spoken . . . but never mind that. Get on out of here and go back to your crib. And be sure nobody sees you leave here. I've got a reputation to protect."

———————◆———————

When she was with Lybrand she was like a girl again—even thought of herself as one, not as the weary, prematurely aging harlot she really was. Only in his company could she dream. As a child and young woman she had dreamed a lot, building cloud castles in which she played out an idealized future. Now, most of the time, she tried not to think of such things. She was worthless, and worthless women had no right to dream of good things. Their only right was escape—through alcohol, opium, suicide. So Dutch Polly Coots had come to believe.

But with Lybrand she had learned to hope again. Particularly at the beginning, when he had treated her so finely and talked to her like a man talks to a beloved wife. He had told her his secrets, outlined his plans... and though it had initially shocked her to find that a man who professed to be a minister was actually preparing to swindle his own church and the local bank as well, she had quickly overlooked it. Let him be what he wants, do what he wants, she thought, as long as he lets me be with him.

Lately, though, it had not always been pleasant to be with him. Lybrand had become cold to Polly— sometimes more than cold. That scared her, but she tried to dismiss his manner as preoccupation with the coming consummation of the scheme he had set up with his two partners, who had come with him from Illinois: the big man named Clure Daugherty and the smaller, weaselly one whose name Polly could never remember. She didn't like those men, didn't trust them. Lately, when they had been around, they had acted jumpy and overeager, accusing Lybrand of stringing them along too long. Polly was afraid they might actually hurt Lybrand.

When she thought about that, sometimes she tried

to pray for Lybrand's safety, though she didn't know if God heard the prayers of girls of the line. She wasn't the same innocent, gentle woman who had once prayed and sung over a baby's crib and tucked quilts up under a little chin. God had heard her then, and loved her. Now she was sure she was beyond receiving love from anyone who was good, especially God.

At least she had Lybrand. Sometimes Polly could almost believe he was the righteous man he pretended to be. His congregation certainly believed in him. He was faithful in visiting the sick, gentle with children, proper in his public manner and words. He preached a fine sermon, too; Polly had once slipped in the back of his tent church to hear him. His voice had been a ship on a billowing ocean: rising, falling, rolling mesmerizingly onward. She had closed her eyes just to enjoy the music of it. When the sermon was over she had slipped quickly out, and the next time she was with him at his cabin he beat her for having dared show herself in his congregation. That was the first time he had lifted a hand to strike her. Sadly, it had not been the last.

A commotion ahead of her on the road caught her attention and held it. It was a man, woman, and child, riding a wagon toward town. The expression on the man's face was one of either great anger or great fear. The woman seemed only half conscious, and there was blood in her hair. She clung to a child on the seat beside her and seemed addled. Polly wondered if the man driving the wagon, probably the woman's husband, had beaten her.

When the wagon drew nearer, Polly noticed that the man seemed a bit addled himself and had blood drying on the sides and back of his neck. He was doing a poor job of driving, steering the horse team too far one way and then too far the other. The wagon came on more quickly than Polly had anticipated, and suddenly veered toward her. She gasped and stumbled back, barely avoiding being overrun.

"Out of my way, whore!" Orv Brown shouted at her as the wagon grumbled past.

Polly felt her face turn red and warm. She had little pride left, and had long ago faced the fact she had become exactly what the man had called her—but something in the way he had said it stirred a smoldering remnant of pride inside her.

"I was a decent woman once, you know!" she yelled after the man, who now was too far away to hear her over the rumbling wagon. "I was respectable, I was!"

She wheeled and began stalking angrily away. A few feet later she stopped and pivoted, yelling, "And I'll be married soon, married to a preacher! You wait and see if'n he don't marry me!"

She threw back her head and continued on toward the prostitute crib that was her home. "You just wait and see if'n he don't!" she repeated herself, because saying it felt good.

───────◆◆───────

Cochran had continued to wander through the town after losing track of the man and boy. He hoped he would run across Frogg, but so far he had found no sign of him.

He was far across town at the time Viola walked in from the mountains, so he did not learn of the incident at once. But word of Snow Sky's newest arrival, who appeared destined to move soon to more celestial quarters, spread across town like smoke on a wind. Cochran was in a saloon having a sandwich and beer when he overheard talk of it.

"And the deputy said his name is Viola," a man at the bar was saying. "He was somebody the preacher Lybrand was looking for. He was beat near to one solid bruise and the marshal figures he's going to die. But they got the man who did it locked up. Name of Frogg."

Cochran drew a lot of attention as he choked on his sandwich. The men at the bar turned and looked at him. "You all right, mister?"

Cochran managed to slide the last bite down his constricted throat. "Yes, yes. I'm fine, thank you."

The man turned and briefly related to his friends more details of the story of Viola's strange arrival and pitiful state. The event was recent enough that so far it had not been corrupted significantly in passage. Cochran tried not to show further visible reaction to the story, but hearing of Frogg's involvement made his knees tremble beneath the table.

He left the rest of his sandwich, paid for his meal, and rushed out. Outside he walked down the street about a block and went into an alley, where he leaned against a wall to collect himself. At last he straightened his shoulders, adjusted his trousers, took a deep breath, and headed for the marshal's office with as much calm and dignity as he could muster.

Frogg jailed as a suspect in a beating? That would certainly explain his absence—though Cochran could not figure out just why Frogg would have been arrested.

Then he remembered the New Testament they had found on the road, and Frogg's insistence he be the one to carry it. A lucky charm, Frogg had hoped it would be. Luck it certainly had brought him, but not the kind he wanted.

Cochran arrived at the marshal's office and three times tried to clear his throat of a lump the size of one of Flory's biscuits. A moment later Cobb opened the door.

"Hello, Marshal," Cochran said, hoping he sounded calm.

The marshal was looking intently at Cochran, trying to place him. Now he remembered: This was the man who had been with Hiram Frogg in the Rose and Thorn Restaurant last night. Interesting he should show up now. He stepped back and let Cochran enter. Cochran took off his hat and felt uncomfortable.

Frogg was seated in a wooden chair beside the marshal's desk, looking like he faced a death sentence. At the moment, with the marshal's attention diverted to Cochran, Frogg gave a flash of his eye and an urgent wiggle of his finger, obviously trying to send a silent message. Cochran wasn't sure what Frogg was trying to convey, but in desperate guesswork he interpreted it as: *Don't link yourself to me. Don't get tied in. Lie like the devil.*

"I met you at a restaurant last night," Cobb said to Cochran. "I'm Earl Cobb. Remember me?"

"Yes. How are you, Mr. Cobb?"

"Just fine. I think you also know my other guest, here."

Cochran looked at Frogg. "Why, yes. We met coming into town," he said. "Decided to share a restaurant meal. Good day to you . . . Mr. Frogg, isn't it? I'm Tudor Cochran, in case my name has slipped your mind."

Frogg said hello.

Cochran looked at the marshal. The innkeeper was not a liar by either nature or practice, and he hoped he would do a good enough job of it now. "I came to report a problem," he said. "I didn't mean to interrupt Mr. Frogg's business with you."

"Mr. Frogg's business is likely to linger for some time," Cobb said. "What's the problem?"

"I saw a drunk strike another with a bottle late last night. I think the man may have been hurt. I should have reported it sooner, I realize."

Cobb blinked. "Is that all?"

"Well, yes."

The marshal chuckled. "Welcome to Snow Sky, Mr. Cochran. You'll see far worse than that before you've been long in this town."

"Oh." Cochran feigned mild confusion. "So you're not interested in the attack I saw?"

"Drunks hitting drunks happens all the time. I can't worry over that. I've got a more significant attack on my mind at the moment."

Good. Cochran had hoped he could steer the conversation around to Frogg's situation. He put on a frown. "Someone attacked Mr. Frogg?"

"The other way around, I suspect. I've got a nearly dead preacher laid up on a cot, and Mr. Frogg had the preacher's New Testament in his pocket."

Cochran said, "Oh, my."

"I'm glad you came in, Mr. Cochran," Cobb said. "I've been asking Mr. Frogg some questions about you, given that you two were together in the restaurant when I first saw you. Did I hear you say you only met him on the edge of town?"

The lump in Cochran's throat grew to two-biscuit size. He feared his voice would fail him, so he simply nodded, praying that his lie matched whatever story Frogg had told.

"How far outside town?"

"Not far at all. At the very edge. We both went for the same restaurant and decided to share company."

"I see." There was a long uncomfortable pause. "Well, Mr. Frogg tells me the same story." Cochran almost collapsed with relief.

Cobb continued. "A good thing for you, really. I might have had to hold you, too, if I suspected you were with him for much time. Tell me, Mr. Cochran— did you see anything peculiar? Any sign that violence had been done to someone along the road?"

"No, Marshal. Nothing."

Cochran cast a side glance at Frogg, beginning to feel guilty. Through a mix of lying and luck he apparently had cleared himself of immediate suspicion, but in so doing had left Frogg without any good alibi. Yet Cochran was sure he had read Frogg's silent signals for deception accurately, and the fact that Frogg himself obviously had already lied to the marshal showed he was trying to keep Cochran in the clear. Cochran wished desperately that he and Frogg could talk privately.

The office door opened and Heck Carpenter walked in. "I told Lybrand about his friend," he announced. "I think he's going to go see him."

The marshal had turned when the door opened; Frogg took advantage of the moment to dig a tight little ball of paper from under his cuff and drop it on the floor. It rolled to Cochran's feet. As the marshal turned, Cochran dropped his hat and stooped to pick it up. When he rose he had the paper as well as the hat.

"Mr. Cochran, since you two tell the same tale about meeting up, I don't have any cause to detain you. But I would appreciate it if you would stay in these parts for a time. I may want to talk to you further. Why are you in town, anyway?"

"An errand for my wife." Cochran blushed; the answer sounded inadequate and unconvincing.

"I see," Cobb said. "Stay around for a bit, you hear?"

Cochran's knees were shaking again. "Certainly, Marshal. Well, I'll go now," Cochran said. "And I'll not report any more attacks unless they appear severe."

"A good policy in Snow Sky," Cobb said. "Otherwise you'd be reporting to me all the time."

Cochran left and walked around a corner, where he sank to his haunches. Got to get a new place to stay, he thought. Can't be registered in the same room as Hiram. Can't have that marshal eyeing me all the time.

He remembered the paper, still clutched in his hand. Quickly he unrolled it. It was a note, obviously written earlier by Frogg to be slipped to Cochran whenever the opportunity arose. It simply said:

Tuder you got to git me cleer of this because if that preecher dies I wil git hungg. Find out who dun it but dont git yourself cawt.
                                                        Hiram F.

Lybrand was at the office door when Hillyer answered. The young preacher's face was pale; he looked terribly worried.

"Is he here?" Lybrand asked.

"Yes." Hillyer's own face was drawn and tight. "You're welcome to come in if you like—I could use the relief. It appears that around here when a man volunteers the use of his office, he's expected to keep it open as a hospital." Hillyer stopped, suddenly looking ashamed. "I'm sorry, Reverend. Pardon that little outburst."

"I understand. Why don't you step out for a walk? I'll sit with Brother Viola. Later I'll arrange to have him brought to my home, where I can tend him until he's well."

Hillyer looked grateful. "You're a good man, Reverend. A walk would do me some good."

When Hillyer was gone, Lybrand took a deep breath, steadied himself, and walked to the back room. He looked down unsmiling upon the pitiful man in the cot.

Viola's eyes opened slowly. When he saw Lybrand standing over him, he blanched, squeaking in an attempt to shout, pulling back on the cot as far as he could.

Lybrand bent over and looked into the gaunt face. "Hello, old man. It appears I didn't do quite as effective a job on you as I thought. I'm impressed with your toughness, I'll admit." He smiled. "Oh, but you've missed one fine performance on my part these last hours. Did you know that after our little encounter outside town, I myself went to the law and told them you hadn't shown up, and that I was worried about you?

Clever, you must admit. That would throw the best law-hound off my scent."

Lybrand's expression became darker, more terrible. "You are a fool, old man—you and your flair for drama, your idiot letters saying you were coming here to strike me down. Were you trying to frighten me? Did you think I was trembling at the fear of you? I've never been afraid of you, old man."

Viola raised a weak arm toward Lybrand, as if to grasp his throat, but Lybrand grabbed the arm and twisted it painfully. Viola made more terrible noises in his injured larynx and squeezed his eyes shut in pain.

"Suffering, are you? Well, not to worry. What I didn't complete on the road I'll finish now. You can walk through your blessed pearly gates and tell all the heavenly host about how evil I am and how you went to your death for the sake of your dishonored little girl. You know, old man, you were the closest thing I've had to a father since my real father died. The same endless religious jabber, self-righteous nonsense. . . . I'm going to do to you what I have wished a thousand times I could have done to him."

Lybrand pulled the worn feather pillow from beneath Viola's head and mashed it into his victim's face. He held it tight. Viola, struggling, grasped by chance the crucifix hanging around Lybrand's neck; he squeezed it until his hand went limp and flopped down to the bunk. Even after that, Lybrand kept the pillow over Viola's face for a long time.

When Hillyer returned, he found Lybrand seated in a chair in the corner of his office. Tears streamed down the young man's face. The cross around his neck glinted in sunlight through the window.

"He's gone," Lybrand said shakily.

"Gone? You mean dead?"

"Yes." Lybrand dabbed at a tear. "A hand more powerful than his has taken him to his reward."

Chapter 5

Earl Cobb withdrew his hand from P. D. Viola's pulseless neck and wiped his fingers on his trousers. "Dead, all right. Sorry about it, Reverend Lybrand. It's a tragedy, it surely is. Did he have family?"

Lybrand, his eyes still rimmed with red, shook his head. He was nervously fingering the crucifix around his neck. "That is probably the only blessing in this situation," he said. "He had no family remaining at all. That's why he felt called to join me here at Snow Sky—he was perfectly fitted to carry on God's work in a mining camp."

"You say he just expired on you while you were visiting him?"

"That's right."

"Did he make any sounds you could interpret, or write any words?"

"No."

Cobb nodded. "Too much to hope for, I suppose.

But it would have helped cinch a conviction if he could have identified our man."

Lybrand looked with interest at Cobb. "Yes. I understand you've got someone jailed already as a suspect?"

"Man name of Frogg. Typical sort of shiftless type. I had him pegged as harmless. Guess that shows I'm not as good a judge of character as I had thought." Lybrand fancied that Cobb cast a deliberate glance at him as he said that, but he wasn't certain. "In any case, that was the dead reverend's Bible in Frogg's pocket. I can't quite figure out why he would have kept that, of all things."

Lybrand asked, "Was Reverend Viola robbed?" He knew the answer full well—he had robbed his victim himself to make robbery appear the motive.

"He was," Cobb answered. "Though I didn't find any money in Frogg's pockets. Maybe he lost it all at the poker table."

"Probably so," Lybrand said. He sighed and wiped his eyes again. "The criminal mind is a tragedy of the fall, is it not?"

"It's a source of never-ending trouble, is what it is. Well, Reverend Lybrand, I'm going to leave it to you to notify any who need to be told of his passing. Where did he live?"

"Chicago."

"That's your old area, too, ain't it?"

"Yes it is. I knew Brother Viola for quite some time there."

Cobb said, "Now if you'll step out a moment, I want to give the body a last examination."

Lybrand looked concerned. "Why?"

"Standard practice. I'll need to be able to testify

about the state of the body when we put Mr. Frogg on trial."

"I see." Lybrand gave his crucifix another twist; tears rolled again down his cheeks. "Such a tragic thing," he said. "Killed in the course of God's work."

"It's a cruel land God has given us to live in," Cobb said. "I suppose he's got his reasons, but you'd know more about that than I would. Good day, Reverend Lybrand."

Lybrand left, closing the door behind him. Cobb looked after him thoughtfully for a moment, his brows lowered above his pale eyes. Had that been whiskey he had smelled on Lybrand's breath? Surely not; Lybrand was famous for his raging anti-liquor sermons. Still, Cobb had always felt somehow that Lybrand was not all he appeared to be. Well, he thought, maybe I'm just too suspicious about mining town preachers. He turned to the body of Viola.

Kneeling, he began at the top of Viola's head and worked down. He got no farther than the nose when he saw something that interested him. He put his head near Viola's chin and looked closely at the dead man's left nostril. Pulling a pencil from his vest pocket, Cobb extended it slightly into the nostril and pulled out a bit of fluffy white. A tiny feather. He then examined the pillow; indeed, it was torn and leaking feathers. But Viola surely had been on his back the entire time he had been on that pillow; he had certainly been in no shape to roll himself over. How had he managed to inhale a feather?

Cobb examined the man further. The more he looked, the more amazed he became that Viola had been able even to make it into town from the woods.

Whoever had beaten him had done so brutally, and surely had believed Viola dead at the end of it.

On impulse, Cobb examined Viola's hands, wondering if there was evidence the preacher had struck or scratched his attacker. The long, supple hands were delicate-looking, and had unbroken fingernails and few calluses. But in the palm of the left hand was a strange red mark, an impression of a shape. Cobb looked closely at it.

He went into Hillyer's empty office and got a paper from the desk. Returning to Viola's side, he carefully sketched the hand and the impression on it. He put the feather on the paper and folded it up inside, and put the paper in his pocket.

Pulling a blanket across the face of the dead man, Cobb left to find the local gravedigger.

Cochran's hand trembled a little as he wrote, and he felt so depressed he worried he might blubber like a woman and wet the paper with tears. He didn't want that, for Flory surely would notice.

My Dear Flory,
     There has been trouble here and I know no soft and easy way to tell you. The Preacher Viola who was with us now is dead and Hiram stands suspected of being his killer, though he is innocent. From what I can pick up the preacher was attacked somewhere along the road into Snow Sky and managed to make his way, in terrible condition, into town on foot. I

suppose his horse was took or run off into the woods.

I know Hiram to be guiltless, but fear there is nothing I can testify that will convince others. Hiram is suspected because he had in his pocket the New Testament of Preacher Viola, but that we had found on the road and Frogg had kept with the plan to give it to the preacher when ever we saw him. This I could tell the marshal, perhaps, but I am sure he would not believe me, for I am new here and unknown to him, and it would be thought that I only was trying to protect my friend. At the moment Hiram and I are pretending to have no real mutual acquaintance and that we merely met at the edge of Snow Sky, but I do not know whether the marshal believes that because he saw us together in a restaurant the night we reached town. I am hoping he will put that down to the common friendliness of two traveling strangers.

Flory, I must remain here to find a way to help Hiram. I do not know what I will do, but I must do something.

I have seen the man and the boy and both look to be fine. Perhaps it will make you feel better about them to know that when I saw them the man was buying the boy shoes, so perhaps he is a good man after all and cares for the boy.

Flory, I will write you again as soon as I have new word to give. Do not worry for me. I do not think the marshal believes I was involved in the death of the preacher, though it is always possible he could begin to think

that way if he perceives Hiram and me as
friends. Hiram at the moment wants me to
continue saying I do not know him, and so I
shall.

    I will be well and hope to be home soon.
Perhaps by the time you read this all will be
set right.

      Your loving husband,
      Tudor

He sealed the letter into an envelope, addressed
it, and mailed it. After that he walked around aimlessly
for a long time, feeling utterly helpless, and wondered
what he could do to help Frogg.

Perhaps he should talk to an attorney, who might
be able to present his evidence more convincingly. But
what evidence? He had nothing but his word—and
now, rightly or wrongly, he and Frogg both had lied to
the law. He again wished desperately he could talk
privately to Frogg.

He continued walking about, thinking. Without
real intention to do so, he gravitated toward the jail,
approaching from the back. In Jail Alley, he leaned
against the wall outside the place where he figured
Frogg's windowless cell was. Wishing for some way to
communicate with his friend, in frustration he picked at
the chinking between the logs.

To his surprise, a big piece of it fell away. He gaped
at it a moment, looked around, and then knelt and
began digging at the remaining chinking. In only a
moment he had made a small hole all the way through.
The jail, it appeared, was built no better than most

mining town buildings. Cochran peered into it, and saw a familiar eye looking back into his.

"Tudor!" Frogg scolded in a whisper through the hole. "You're going to get yourself hung like me doing such fool truck as this!"

"I had to talk to you, Hiram. This is the only way." Cochran looked fearfully around, hoping no one who passed the alley would look into it. "You know how bad's the trouble we're in?"

"What do you mean, we? It's my tail in the sling!"

"Your problem, my problem. I'm the one who asked you to come to Snow Sky."

"And I'm the one who insisted on carrying that Bible. Tudor, you know I didn't kill that preacher. But there's no way we'll convince the law of that."

"We shouldn't have lied," Cochran whispered back. "I should have come out from the beginning and said I know you and that we were together."

"No! That would just have landed you in here with me. You got to stay free, Tudor. You got to find something to clear my name."

"What, for gosh sake?"

"Find who really killed the preacher."

"How? I'm no detective. I don't know how to dig up information like that!"

"Then find somebody who can." There was a pause. "Shhh! Somebody coming!"

Then Cochran could tell Frogg had moved away from the little hole. Thinking quickly, Cochran scooped up a bit of the broken-out chinking and stuffed it back into the hole so that no flash of sunlight from the outside would betray the opening to the jailers. Then, feeling more despairing than before, Cochran walked away, shoulders slumped. Though the sun beamed down on the active town of Snow Sky, Cochran saw nothing but various shades of dark gray.

Lybrand took a long, deep slug of whiskey, followed by a longer, deeper breath. He looked at his hand. Trembling. That would not do. A good actor never loses his nerve. Just keeps playing his scenes until the show is through.

He rose and walked about his cabin until he had calmed a bit. This had turned into a nastier business than he had anticipated. He wished he had done a more efficient job the first time he had tried to rid himself of Viola. But how could he have guessed the old devil could have survived such a vicious beating as he had given him? By all rights, Viola should have marched skyward for whatever rewards awaited him, rather than coming like an ambulant cadaver into Snow Sky to demand even more lethal attention.

Well, at least he was gone now, and this time without question. Lybrand took another drink, feeling very tense, though also somewhat relieved. Viola had been a thorn in his side for a long time, the worst Lybrand had ever been stuck with. Being the man he was, Lybrand had dealt with a lot of enemies, but never had he fully understood what an enemy really was until he had been faced with a father angered by a daughter's lost honor. He also had never had to kill before, and though he was glad to know he had the grit to do it, it had left him feeling tight, ready to snap.

A knock on his door... Lybrand almost dropped

his whiskey bottle trying to hide it. His breath—surely he reeked of liquor. Quickly he filled and lit a pipe, hoping the strong tobacco odor would mask the alcohol. After a few furious puffs, he went to the door and opened it.

It was Dutch Polly, the crib girl. She grinned crookedly. "Ain't you going to invite a poor girl in?"

Lybrand swore in a tense whisper and looked furtively around. Seeing no one else around, he grabbed her by the shoulder, pulled her roughly inside, and slammed the door behind her.

"You're hurting me!" she protested.

Lybrand slapped her across the face, hard. She screeched and pulled away.

"Oh! It hurts!" She cowered into a crouch before him. "Don't hit me, Jason, don't!"

"Very well," he said. He drew back his foot and kicked her, sending her sprawling.

Pointing a long finger down at her, he said, "Don't you ever come around to my front door, especially in daylight, you hear? Do you know what it would do to me if I were seen with the likes of you? You're not supposed to come at all except at the arranged times!"

"I just thought—"

His tension boiled into fury; he poured it on her at full temperature. "You're not fit to think. You're fit to do only one thing—and even that's becoming more trouble than pleasure. More trouble than you're worth."

Polly began crying. Her fantasy that Lybrand cared seriously for her was being beaten to death before her eyes. She looked up at him, rubbing her reddened face. "Don't talk to me like that, Jason! I can't bear to hear it!"

"Why did you come here?"

"I . . . wanted to be with you."

"When I want you around, I'll let you know."

"This time it wasn't for what you wanted that I came—I came for myself, just to be near you. Don't you understand that? I'm a woman, Jason. I have feelings."

"You're a crib girl, and crib girls can't afford feelings."

Lybrand looked silently at her as she cried. He had just experienced an unwelcome realization: Dutch Polly was in love with him. He couldn't imagine a more unwanted development. Here he was, thriving in his clerical masquerade, only today rid at last of the long-searching, daughter-avenging P. D. Viola—and now he had a common prostitute in love with him. Sometimes it was terribly inconvenient to be a good-looking man; Dutch Polly wasn't the first of her breed to decide Lybrand was worthy of more than physical affection.

He decided to take a softer approach with her. "You may think you love me, Polly, but you don't. Neither one of us knows a thing about love. That can't be part of your world or mine, and I, for one, am content with that. You need to learn to be the same." He dug into his pocket and pulled out a couple of coins. He tossed them to the crouching young woman's feet. "Take it. Learn to get your happiness from that. That's the only thing you could ever really love, and the only god I could every worship. Neither one of us can afford to take what we offer seriously. Far better to be a seller than a buyer."

Polly, who felt as if her entire world was being knocked off its course, only cried harder, and pleaded, "No, Jason, please don't do this! I know I shouldn't have come, but I couldn't help it!"

His expression and voice grew cold. "In that case, you're getting out of control, and that makes you dangerous to me. I won't have you behaving in a way that threatens my interests."

Suddenly her grief turned to anger, and she scratched at him. He substantially evaded her, receiving only a scratch on his cheek, then threw out a fist and struck her in the mouth. She fell, lip bleeding.

He swore and grabbed his hand; he had slightly cut his knuckle on one of her yellowed teeth. A little drop of blood trickled down from the scratch on his cheek and dripped to the floor.

"Out!" he ordered. "Out before I snap your pimply neck!"

She was drying her tears on her sleeve; now she wiped her nose along the underside of it. "You can't talk so to me!" she declared. "I'm a lady, not some dog for you to spit on."

"You're a bit less than a dog, my dear, and far less than a lady. Get out—and go the back way. I won't need your services again—don't come around here any-more."

She stumbled toward his back door. As she left she turned. "You haven't heard the last of me," she said. "I wonder what the good people who hear you preach would think to know what you really are? How they'd like to know their preacher's dealings with Dutch Polly? How'd they like somebody to tell them that their preacher and two common thieves are planning to steal their offering plate money right out from under their noses?"

He glowered and stepped forward. "Don't threaten me!" he bellowed. She closed the door and cut him off.

He went to it and threw it open, started to yell after her. He realized suddenly he could not do that.

The Reverend Jason Lybrand could hardly afford to be seen shouting after a crib girl.

Cursing, he slammed the door. Another little drop of blood oozed from his cut knuckle and dripped on the floor.

The next time someone knocked at the door, Lybrand opened it and found Earl Cobb. The false preacher uttered a quick and very uncharacteristic prayer of gratitude that he hadn't taken a drink in the last hour. Cobb was the sort who could detect that kind of thing.

"Marshal!" he said. "A pleasant surprise—come in." *What has Polly gone and said?* he wondered desperately. But his concern did not show on his face.

Cobb said, "I don't have long to stay, Preacher, but I wanted to ask you to conduct the burial service for your friend Viola tomorrow morning, ten o'clock. We need to get him under quick, with the weather getting warmer."

Lybrand felt great relief; this was just a routine call by the marshal after all. "Yes. I would have been happy to have conducted the services today, Marshal, if that would have been better."

"I couldn't have obliged you, Parson," Cobb said. "I was busy with the body of the deceased. Examination, you know. And then there was a robbery this morning. Orv Brown and his wife. Members of your congregation, ain't they?"

"Yes. Are they all right?" Lybrand was seriously interested . . . in Kimmie Brown, not Orv.

"A little battered, but nothing serious."

"Thank God. I will have to call on them. Your

examination of Brother Viola's body—did you find anything?"

"Just a bit of evidence." Cobb paused, a bit too long. Lybrand felt his heart jump. "I need all that I can get to see that proper justice is dispensed to Mr. Frogg," Cobb continued.

"Yes. Of course. Thanks for coming, Marshal. Ten in the morning, you say?"

"Right, and I thank you," Cobb said. He lifted his chin and looked down his nose at Lybrand's face. "You know, Preacher, you got a scratch there. If you weren't a man of the cloth I'd swear you'd been scrapping with a long-nailed female." Cobb's eyes flickered to look into Lybrand's for a moment, then the marshal laughed.

Lybrand looked unsettled, then also laughed. "Marshal, you're a rather irreverent fellow," he said. "Believe it or not, I like a touch of that in a man. It reminds us men of the cloth not to become too pompous. As for that scratch, I got it from a scrape against a protruding nail this afternoon. Careless construction around here, you know."

"Well, that's a relief. I'd hate to think Snow Sky's only man of the cloth had to be watched to make sure he wasn't violating any commandments," Cobb responded, giving Lybrand another piercing look that did not escape the preacher's notice. Cobb touched his hat. "So long, Parson, and again accept my sorrow for the passing of your friend."

"Thank you."

As Earl Cobb walked away, he could feel Lybrand's stare. He smiled; his little attempt to unsettle the preacher had worked. He had seen Lybrand's moments of uncertainty, of feverish, quick study of the loaded words he had pitched out. Cobb had played a suspicion and found the results rewarding, if somewhat disturbing.

Back in his office, Cobb sent Heck Carpenter to the Rose and Thorn to fetch a couple of plates of food and, after Heck was gone, unfolded a paper from his pocket and studied by lamplight the tiny feather that had been enclosed, and the sketch of Viola's hand and the peculiar mark upon it. Part of the reason he had gone to Lybrand's just now had been to make a surreptitious comparison of the mark—which looked remarkably like the imprint of a small cross in the dead man's palm—and the crucifix that hung around Lybrand's neck.

Back in his cell, Hiram Frogg snored, sounding like one of Snow Sky's lumber mills. Cobb rose and quietly walked back to the wall of square-crossed flat iron bars and looked at the sleeping man. After a few moments he went back to his desk and sat down again.

Preacher Lybrand, he thought, I think I'll be watching you right close for the next little bit. Right close indeed.

———————◆◆◆———————

Lybrand really was edgy now. Cobb had stirred him so, with his peculiar and seemingly knowing words, that he felt endangered. He loaded his derringer, slipped it into his frock coat pocket, and left the cabin, intent upon a walk.

Did Cobb suspect him? Surely not. Cobb was nothing but a small-time mountain marshal, nothing like the well-trained police and Pinkerton men Lybrand had dealt with back in Chicago. Yet Cobb could unsettle him with nothing more than a glance and a change of tone.

Lybrand strode by night toward the northern edge of Snow Sky, keeping in the darkest places all the way. By the flare lights on the street he watched people moving about. At times, when he kept his gaze low and ignored the squatty skyline and the dirt avenues, this place reminded him of some of Chicago's seamier portions, where he had grown up, learning to scrap and fight and hate and devote himself to one cause: improving his own lot at any cost required.

"Howdy, Preacher."

Lybrand was startled; the voice had emerged from the darkness to his right. A glowing red spot, bouncing about six feet above the ground, flared and came toward him. It was the coal of a cigar riding on the lip of a tall, bristle-bearded miner named Corbin Bottoms. Bottoms was built like a small mountain and had features as battered and weathered as the undersides of the federal naval vessels upon which he had served, underage, during the long-past civil hostilities. Rough as he looked, he was as gentle and decent a soul as Snow Sky could boast; even Lybrand had recognized that.

"Hello, Corbin."

"Y'hear 'bout Orv and Kimmie Brown?"

"Yes. Just a few moments ago. Terrible thing."

"Yep. Him and Kimmie both got knocked in the head, but they're not bad hurt. Everybody's talking about it."

"Yes. Good night, Corbin." The preoccupied Lybrand started to walk away. But Bottoms still wanted to talk.

"It was two men what done it. Sacks over their heads to hide them. But one had a real soft way of talking, Orv says. High-pitched. Orv says he'll know that voice when he hears it."

Lybrand frowned. "Soft way of talking?"

"Yep. Well, g'night, preacher."

"Good night, Corbin."

The big man took the cigar into his hand and walked away; the red glow of the cigar receded and vanished.

Lybrand swore aloud when Bottoms was gone. A big man with a high-pitched, soft voice—that sounded like Clure Daugherty. And if it was, the other robber surely must have been Ivan Dade.

Lybrand knew his partners had been growing restless, and Daugherty even had dropped a hint that he might undertake a venture or two on his own if Lybrand did not give a go-ahead soon on the plan they had worked out together. Lybrand had not taken that seriously; Daugherty was always one for big talk. He had made such threats all the years he and Lybrand had worked together in everything from common theft and burglary to sophisticated confidence schemes. The threats had always proven idle.

But now he might actually have put action into his words and, if so, had endangered Lybrand's plan.

Problems upon problems: Dutch Polly making threats, Daugherty and Dade foolishly acting on their own, a town marshal growing suspicious...

Lybrand turned on his heel and headed back toward his home. He needed a drink, bad.

Chapter 6

It had been a very frustrating day. Cochran had roamed the streets of Snow Sky for hours, trying to think of some way to help Frogg, and nothing had come to mind. At last he had gone back to his new rented room and tried to sleep, but sleep would not come. Almost angrily he had jumped out of bed and now was out in town again, walking back and forth up Mud Street, stomping along the Silver Street boardwalk, cutting from alley to alley in purposeless frustration under the light of the street flares.

At the moment he walked in an unlighted area near the Dixie Lee Dance Hall, which stood off the main streets behind a row of stores. On the far side was a thick patch of woods. Raucous music from a brass band poured from inside the big tent that housed the dance hall. Cochran thought about going in to attempt to brighten his spirits, but hesitated to do so, for he had heard someone say the Dixie Lee was the most notorious center for prostitution in all of Snow Sky, and

Cochran didn't care for that sort of thing. His father had spent a good deal of time back during Cochran's Alabama childhood warning his son off strong drink, fighting, and bad women, and it had stuck. The truth was, women had always frightened Cochran a little, except for Flory. Flory he was fully at ease with, and never fully at ease without.

Something moved behind Cochran, startling him—then suddenly a dark, seemingly huge form lunged directly at him, and a strong arm crooked around his neck. He found himself held from the rear in a stranglehold. A voice, filtered through gritted teeth, spoke directly into his right ear. Cochran's glasses sat pinched at a cocked angle on his nose.

"Why were you following me?"

Cochran shifted his eyes and tried to turn his head; the stranglehold tightened. "You know who I am, innkeeper! Why did you follow me here?"

Now Cochran did know, and his legs went weak, but only for a moment. He was the sort of man who occasionally surprised other people, sometimes even himself. So it was now. With an almost random wrench of his body and gouge of his elbow, he pulled free from the arm that held him, and at the same time pounded his assailant in the stomach. The man's breath burst out and he staggered back.

Cochran spun on his heel, straightened his glasses, and took on a boxing pose that would have brought forth a roaring laugh from Frogg, had he been there to see it. His attacker didn't laugh; Cochran had actually hurt him.

"Didn't expect that from you, innkeeper," the man admitted. "You don't look the sort."

"Don't attack me again," Cochran said.

"Then tell me why you're in Snow Sky following me around."

Cochran lowered his fists. "I'll tell you if you'll tell me who you are."

The man paused, obviously trying to remember the name he had signed on the inn register. "Joe Jackson," he finally said.

"Really? You signed in as John at the inn."

"Then I'm John Jackson. What does it matter to you?"

"It doesn't matter to me very much at all, sir. But it does matter to my wife. She's worried about the welfare of the boy you had with you—and don't tell me he's your son. Flory knew from looking that he's not kin to you, and she's always been able to tell such things."

The man stepped forward and put out a finger. He was tall, with dark hair, a ruggedly handsome, wind-browned face, and a beard that reminded Cochran of Ulysses Grant's. The only light here was what filtered out through the dance hall tent wall, so Cochran couldn't at the moment see the man's face clearly, but even so the intensity of the black eyes was evident. "What business is this of yours?" the bearded man asked.

"None, I suppose. But I've had a very bad day, and at the moment I'm not all that concerned about what is my business and what isn't. I followed you because my wife worried for the boy. Maybe that's not my affair. Maybe it is."

The man was obviously dissatisfied with the answer. "You're lying. Nobody would follow a stranger just because of some boy."

"It's obvious you don't know Flory Cochran. She

happens to care a lot about children—and for some reason, about this child in particular."

The man was acting more cautious. "Do you know me?" he demanded.

Cochran felt he could best keep his advantage by bluffing. "Maybe I have some suspicions. Where's the boy?"

The man looked silently at Cochran for a time. "He's fine. Safe. You needn't worry about him."

"Who is he?"

"Just a boy." The man glowered. "You never mind— I'll see to him."

"What does that mean?" Cochran was surprised at his own boldness; he usually did not bear up so well in confrontations.

The man grew angry all at once. He came at Cochran again and grabbed him by the shirt. He pulled Cochran's face close to his. "Leave it be, innkeeper! Stay away from me! Don't follow me, don't ask about me, and don't worry over the boy! Like I said: I'll see to him."

He lifted Cochran off the ground and threw him back. Cochran's spine struck hard against a tree, snapping back his head and making it also pound the trunk. Stars burst against the backlighted luminescence of the canvas dance hall, and for a few moments Cochran was stunned. When his head cleared, the man was gone.

Rising slowly, groaning, Cochran rubbed the back of his head and wandered back toward his room. Only now did he begin to realize how much danger he might have been in.

When Cochran was far from the Dixie Lee, the boy who had so captured Flory Cochran's concern emerged from the place at the edge of the woods where he had been hiding, watching, and listening. He had slipped unseen out of his bed and followed the tall, bearded man, and had taken in all that had just occurred. He looked wistfully in the direction Cochran had gone, but turned and went at a dead run back toward the place where he and his keeper were staying, not wanting it to be known that he had ever left it.

Cobb walked into the jail office and took off his hat. Cap Corley was sipping coffee and cleaning his pistol.

"You get that dead preacher planted?" the deputy asked.

Cobb nodded. "Lybrand said a few words and we put him under. Lybrand cried and slung snot like a spanked baby."

"Guess it would put most anybody into a state, having a fellow who was coming to see you get killed like that."

"Maybe so. But at the same time, Lybrand didn't seem all that sincere to me."

"Well, I can't see why he wouldn't be. I thought this Viola was a good friend who was going to help Lybrand start up a proper church."

"That's the story Lybrand tells, at least."

Cobb walked back to the cellblock. Frogg, seated on his cot, was just finishing off a biscuit and the last of a cup of coffee. A tray with the remnants of his lunch sat on the floor at his feet.

"Right good victuals, Marshal," Frogg said.

"Glad you like 'em. Can we have a talk?"

Frogg leaned back against the wall. "I had a few

previous appointments, but I suppose I can cancel them for you."

Cobb got the key and opened the cell. He sat down on the cot beside Frogg and began rolling a cigarette. "Want one?"

"Don't mind if I do." Frogg borrowed the makings and rolled a smoke for himself as Cobb lit his. Cobb tossed the matches to Frogg, who fired up his own cigarette and tossed them back.

"Mr. Frogg, why don't you tell me exactly what happened the day you came to Snow Sky?"

"I already told you."

"Tell me again."

"All right. I rode toward town, and a little ways out from it I saw this book on the road. It was a little Bible, so I decided to keep it for a good luck charm. Thought it might help me win some poker or faro, you know. I put it in my pocket and there it stayed until you took it out."

"You see anyone?"

"Not until I got to the edge of town and met that Cochran man."

"Think he might have killed Viola?"

The question chilled Frogg, but he didn't let it show. "No."

"Why do you say that?"

"I just don't think he could have done it."

"You were alone before you met him?"

"Yep."

"And you never saw Viola at all?"

"Never laid eyes on him. Haven't to this day," Frogg said.

Cobb mulled it over. He finished his cigarette, crushed it out, picked up Frogg's tray, and stood.

"Marshal, do you believe me?"

Cobb opened the cell and let himself out. He shut it and shook it to make sure the lock had caught. "I'll be honest: I'm having trouble keeping myself convinced you killed that preacher. Can't shake the notion you didn't do it."

Frogg was obviously surprised. "Then why don't you let me out?" he asked.

"Perhaps it will come to that . . . when I know a little more about a few things. There's one more suspect . . . but I need some more to go on." Cobb leaned on the cell door. "I'm tired, Mr. Frogg. Very tired. Robberies in people's home, dead preachers—it's a wearying thing for a man of the law. And it's worse when what you're trying to piece together doesn't seem to fit. There are some pieces of this situation that are misfits for sure."

"What's that mean?"

"If I knew I'd tell you. Right now I'm just talking hunches and feelings. Good day, Mr. Frogg."

Cobb walked out. Frogg finished his cigarette and wished he had another.

The next morning, a sharp rap on the door pulled Cochran out of deep sleep. He sat up in a stupor. More rapping, sharper than before.

Cochran climbed out of bed and put on his pants. Running his fingers through his hair, he answered the door. From the vigor of the knocking he expected to find someone telling him the building was on fire.

At the door he found a short, slender man with short-cropped brown hair and round wire-rimmed glasses. The fellow struck him first as hardly more than a boy, but at second glance Cochran noted wrinkles around the mouth and the corners of the eyes. In the thick brown hair were a few streaks of gray.

"Oliver Byers, sir," the man said, extending his hand. "I'm sorry to have disturbed you—obviously you were sleeping." Byers had a small mouth and cold blue eyes. His voice was as neatly clipped as his hair. Cochran mumbled out his own name and lamely shook the offered hand. Byers continued. "I hope you'll let me take a moment or two of your time."

Cochran, driven by curiosity, hesitantly stepped back and waved Byers inside. He stretched, yawned, and finger-combed his hair again. "Who are you?" he asked.

"I'm the editor of the Snow Sky *Argus,*" Byers said. "I need to talk to you."

Cochran frowned. "What's this about?" With Frogg in jail and himself in a precarious position, he was naturally cautious.

"It's about Abel Patterson."

Abel Patterson? Cochran had never heard of him. "I think you have the wrong man," he said. "I don't know any Patterson."

Byers grinned knowingly. "No? Then why did I see you following him around town yesterday morning? You needn't deny it—I watched you for several minutes."

"So that's his name, huh?" Cochran muttered.

Cochran went to his bed and sat down, wishing for

a cup of coffee and wondering if he should toss Byers out. He rested his elbows on his knees and put his face into his hands. "I don't think I should be talking to you," he said. "I don't know what you have in mind. How'd you find me?"

"I saw you come here earlier." Byers paused, then abruptly asked, "What do you think a newspaper should be?" Cochran looked up at him, bewildered by the question, which carried a menacing hint of a coming lecture on journalism.

"I'll tell you what it should be by telling you first what it shouldn't: It shouldn't be simply a broadsheet for town promoters to boost their developments at the expense of truth. It should be a teller of the hard, bitter truth about a town and the people in it. It should expose secrets, not perpetuate them. I'm from Chicago, Mr. Cochran. I know journalism at its best, not just the throw-away rubbish you see in so many new towns like ours. I came to Snow Sky because I wanted to be part of the excitement of a mining town. I want to show that such a town is best served by a newspaper that doesn't shirk from the facts and doesn't conspire to mask secrets for the sake of some imagined community welfare. And believe me, there are secrets here that merit exposure— Abel Patterson being the newest. Not to mention yourself."

Cochran asked, "Who is Abel Patterson?"

Byers knitted his brows. "You really don't know?"

"I really don't know. I followed him here from the inn I own, but I don't know who he is, and didn't even know his real name until this moment."

"Why did you follow him?"

"What makes that your business?"

"Having the sheer gall to ask, I suppose. Look at it

this way: I've made it my business, and if you want this story handled as it should be, I suggest you tell the truth."

"So now I'm a story, huh?"

"Potentially, yes."

Cochran stared at Byers a few moments. The news-paperman was a problem he didn't need. He played again with the idea of throwing him out, then reconsid-ered. Angering Byers might just make things worse. Maybe it wouldn't hurt to tell him a little of the truth, just enough to satisfy him . . . Cochran hoped. Maybe Byers could give him some information about this Abel Patterson in return.

"I followed him because of my wife."

"Oh! He made improper advances to her?"

That really made Cochran mad. His face reddened. "No. Not at all. You'd have to know my wife to under-stand my reason, Mr. Byers. She worries over folks, especially children." He briefly told Byers about Flory's concerns and his agreement to come check on the boy's welfare. "Perhaps you find that foolish. But it's the truth. Not much of a story, is it?"

But Byers' eyes were gleaming. "So the boy really is with Patterson! Fascinating—I can't figure out that one."

Cochran said, "I've given you what information I have. Now why don't you do the same for me? Just who is Abel Patterson?"

Byers rubbed his chin a moment as if trying to decide how much to tell. He sat down on the room's only chair and crossed his legs. "Abel Patterson is a former Pinkerton agent. He was a good one, too, with an outstanding reputation until a couple of years ago.

He was based in Chicago, in Pinkerton's home office. I became familiar with him through my crime reporting. He was aloof, but the best criminal investigator I've ever seen, with the possible exception of his brother, Roland. He was a Pinkerton too."

"Patterson was a criminal investigator?" Cochran repeated. The seed of a rather bizarre idea immediately planted itself.

"That's right. When he was on a case it would possess him; he would work without sleep or food, hound the truth until he ran it down. The Chicago police would have loved to have the Patterson brothers on their force, but the two of them liked private work. Let me tell you, they made news in Chicago, right up until the day Roland was killed."

"Killed? What happened?"

"He was shot down when he walked into a robbery. A senseless death. He and Abel had been investigating a series of such robberies, and the theory is he had detected a pattern or picked up some hint as to where the next would be. He walked in on it, and bang, he's dead. Abel Patterson happened to be elsewhere that night. It was just one of those tragedies that happens, nobody's fault, but Abel Patterson didn't see it that way. He blamed himself. It brought the end of his career with the Pinkertons.

"Patterson left the agency and went to work on his own, doing jobs far below his level of skill—investigating adultery for divorce cases, serving as a bodyguard for rich men with something to fear from one side of the law or the other. He began to drink a lot. Then one day he was gone. Headed west, the talk was. I saw no more of him after that—not until this week. Here I am, walking down Silver Street, and I look and see Abel Patterson, in the flesh, coming out of a rooming house with a boy at his heel. At first I thought my eyes were fooling me, but I followed him a good while, and sure enough, it was Patterson." Byers smiled. "I also detected at one point that someone else had started following him, too. And not too well, I must add."

"So I'm not a tracker or a detective," Cochran said. "I never claimed to be. Patterson saw me just like you did. Looked right at me."

"Really? Did he react to you, say anything?"

Seeing no reason to reveal the encounter outside the Dixie Lee Dance Hall, Cochran said, "No. Just looked and went on."

"Interesting. Everything about this is interesting— the unexplainable little boy, the money in the bank . . ."

"Money?"

"Yes indeed—big money. I have a contact at the Miner and Merchant Bank. I'm told that Patterson deposited almost fifty thousand dollars there when he arrived in town. And not silver—cash."

"That's a pile of money."

"It is. Where did he get it? Where did he get the boy, and who is he? And why did Patterson come to Snow Sky? He's not the sort to become a miner—or to need to, with the kind of money he's got deposited."

Cochran rolled his shoulders to loosen them. "Got any answers?"

"Not really. I was hoping you might."

"Sorry to let you down."

Byers stood and paced the little room. "The answers will come, if I keep looking for the connections. I learned in Chicago that even in the big city there usually are links between events and people that don't seem to relate on the surface. Surely that is even more true in a smaller town. For example, you're linked to Patterson, and also to the man over in the jail with a murder charge coming his way."

Cochran, feeling the newspaperman now was getting around to his real reason for being here, suddenly grew animated, stood, and reaffirmed the lie he and Frogg had created. "Like I told the marshal, I'm not connected to that man beyond having met him at the edge of town," he said. "I rode in with him and we shared a meal at a restaurant, and that's it."

Byers laughed. "Come now! If that's true, why were you talking into his cell through the jail wall yesterday?"

Cochran wasn't a good enough liar to bluff out of that unexpected challenge. He gaped at Byers. "What right do you have to spy on everyone in town?"

"It's my job. You're a question mark. Another potential story."

"And that's all that matters?"

"To me, yes."

"So are you going to print me up in your newspaper?"

The newspaperman shrugged. "At the moment, no. In the future, maybe. It depends upon what I find."

Cochran didn't know how to react to this man. Byers had already made him mad; Cochran felt toward him like he would toward an oversized maggot.

But he had to admit the information Byers had given him was valuable. An intriguing idea had already grown out of it. He decided to probe Byers a little further.

"Let's quit talking about me for the moment. Tell me more about Patterson," Cochran said.

"No more to tell just yet. At the moment he's just another question mark, like you. And you two are certainly not the only ones. For example, there's another individual in Snow Sky. . . fascinating character, but not what he seems. I'm expecting an entire package of information from some old newspaper friends back in Chicago—should shine some light on him. See what I mean about connections? He's another former Chicago man. That's the way it is in a boom town. There's not a major city in the country that doesn't have at least a score of its folk here."

Byers abruptly changed his manner. He had become relaxed as he talked, but now he went stiff and formal. "Thank you for your time," he said. "I'll talk to you again, I'm sure."

When Byers was gone, clipping off down the street with his spine as straight as a rifle barrel, Cochran went to the mirror and rubbed the stubble on his face. A shave and wash was what he needed—a good clean appearance to help him do a job of persuading a man who would not be inclined to be persuaded. This Abel Patterson, whomever and whatever he might be, surely would find it quite peculiar that the very man he had attacked outside a dance hall in the night would come to him pleading for help. It was a crazy idea Byers had given Cochran—but even a crazy idea seemed better than none.

Cochran poured water from the pitcher into the basin and began to wash his face.

Chapter 7

Kimmie Brown, framed in the doorway of her home, was as pretty as always despite the bandage tied around her forehead. She looked back at Lybrand in surprise. Her child stood at her side, clutching Kimmie's skirt in tight little fists.

"Reverend Lybrand! I wasn't expecting you to call!"

He flashed white, sparkling teeth. "I hope it is no imposition." He looked over her shoulder into the cabin. "Is Orv here?"

"No. He's . . ." She looked uncomfortable and paused.

"Working?"

"No. Not today." She sighed. "He's probably down in town . . . going through the saloons."

Lybrand lifted his left brow. "Drinking?"

"No, thank God. But it's just as bad. We were robbed, and the robbers struck us." She touched her bandage. "Since then Orv has been dead set to find them. He's convinced that if he roams the saloons enough, he can find the robbers."

"I had heard about the robbery," Lybrand said. "In fact, I came to see how all of you came through it. Thank God he spared your lives." Lybrand frowned. "What you say about Orv concerns me, though. I hope he knows what he is doing."

"So do I. I wish he would just let it all go, but—oh! Forgive me! I'm rude to have you still standing at the door, Reverend. Please do come in."

"I don't know if I should, with Orv away. A minister must be careful to avoid even the likeness of, well, impropriety, you know."

"Don't be silly." Kimmie stood aside and gestured for him to come in.

Lybrand did, his saintly expression masking most unsaintly thoughts. Kimmie Brown was one of Snow Sky's most beautiful women, certainly the most attractive in his church. Once again he regretted the personal sacrifices that came with masquerading as a clergyman. If not for the economic value of this deception, he would snatch up Kimmie for his own.

"The robbery—tell me about it," Lybrand said.

Kimmie sat on a stool, arms around her child's shoulders. Briefly she described how it all had happened.

"But if they wore masks, how does Orv think he can recognize the robber?" Lybrand asked.

"One had a strange voice. Very high-pitched. Orv says he would recognize it again. I think I would, too. It was a remarkable voice."

Lybrand frowned in concern that Kimmie took to be for Orv but which in fact simply marked an unwanted confirmation. Kimmie's words had cinched his suspicion that Clure Daugherty had in fact been one of the robbers. Surely the other was Ivan Dade. Lybrand mentally swore at his partners. He didn't need any loose cannons at the moment.

"Will you talk to Orv, Reverend? Try to convince him to forget all this?"

"I'll speak with him, first opportunity." Lybrand stood, feeling the ache that Kimmie always aroused in him. He restlessly fingered the cross hanging on his chest. When his scheme was played out—when he could cast off this pretense and be free of its strictures—then, he vowed to himself, he would come back and take her away with him.

Lybrand said his goodbye and left, trudging down the dirt road into Snow Sky.

Lybrand leaned against a tree near the Dixie Lee Dance Hall, watching people pass, nodding at those he knew from his congregation. "Going to preach you a street sermon?" one asked. Lybrand smiled.

At last he caught the attention of a young boy and called him over. He knelt and whispered to the boy, gave him a coin, showed him another. The boy went to the door of the dance hall and sneaked in. Lybrand waited.

A few minutes later the boy reemerged, Clure Daugherty with him. The boy ran to Lybrand, claimed the other coin, and darted off as Daugherty lumbered over.

"Come on," Lybrand said, not looking directly at Daugherty. "We have to talk."

Together they walked toward a place where a woodshed edged up against a patch of woods. At the front of the shed they were out of potential view from most angles.

"What do you want?" Daugherty said.

"Why the hell did you rob the Orv Brown place?"

Daugherty glared at Lybrand. "Who says I did?"

"I do. A big man with a high voice, they said— you're a fool to not know how easy you are to identify, mask or no mask."

"Don't call me a fool."

"Then don't behave like one. Whose idea was it, anyway? Yours or Dade's?"

Daugherty curled his lip. "Let's just say it was ours together. It's hard to sit in that cabin waiting for you to give word, Jason."

"We've worked together enough years for you to know that patience pays off. You let me get the church's bank account built up high enough, and we'll walk out of that bank with quite a pile. But you try another off-the-cuff robbery or some other damn-fool thing like that, you're liable to wind up dead."

"I can take care of myself."

"Maybe, maybe not. You earned yourself a problem you didn't need when you robbed Orv Brown. Now he's out looking for you. He's got every chance of finding you, too, with that voice of yours. Brown's in my congregation. I know him well enough to tell you he's got more hot temper than religion. He's already looking for you, and he won't quit until he finds you."

That aroused a light of worry in Daugherty's eyes, but he tried to damper it. "He won't find me, and even if he did, I'd take care of him."

"And get yourself jailed for it. You made a big mistake, Daugherty. You endangered our plan."

Daugherty grew angry. "And what about you? Your dallying around with that crib girl's more dangerous to us than anything I've done. And what about this dead preacher everybody's talking about? Viola—that's your old papa-in-law, and don't deny it. He came looking for you, didn't he?"

"Viola's dead. He can't hurt us. It's living and breathing idiots like you and Dade who'll bring everything down."

"Did you kill Viola?"

"There's a man over in the jail they say killed him. As long as he's there it doesn't matter who really did it, does it?"

Clure put a finger against Lybrand's chest. "That's as good as an admission, Jason. Hell, it ain't me and Dade what needs worrying about, it's you! All we done was rob a miner. You kilt a man!"

"Shut up."

"I won't shut up. It's time you hear me out. Seems to me you're taking too many chances. How much have you told that whore of yours, anyway? She know what we're up to?"

Lybrand didn't want to answer, so instead he lost his temper. His right arm shot out and his fist cracked against Daugherty's jaw.

Daugherty spasmed but did not stagger back. His oak-stout form absorbed the blow easily.

With a snarl and an oath, Daugherty pushed forward against Lybrand, knocking him back with the heels of his hands on Lybrand's chest. The false preacher fell back onto the door of the little woodshed. It fell open behind him and he collapsed inside.

A stack of cordwood fell atop him, and then several slabs of lumber. He was buried.

And at once Daugherty, Snow Sky, Viola, Dutch Polly, and everything else of the present was forgotten. Lybrand was back in Chicago, a boy again. He was no longer inside a woodshed, but in a familiar tiny closet. Outside it was his hated, drunken father, holding shut the door and praying loudly above the sound of his claustrophobic son's screams.

Lybrand had hated small, squeezing places almost from the crib. Even as an infant, his mother had once told him, he had writhed out of his blanket whenever he was swaddled. And as a growing child, the horrors that most dominated his nightmares always centered on closeness, enclosure, entrapment. Lybrand's father, a man consumed by both alcohol and a twisted religious zealotry, knew it and called it the work of demons.

"Let me out! Let me out!" Lybrand screamed. "Please, Papa, let me out!"

The prayers of his father, though muffled by the door, seemed loud to him. "Cast the demon from him, Lord! Purge the evil from his soul!"

Then his mother's weary voice: "Let him out, Jim—for God's sake, please let him out!"

"For God's sake, for his sake, I can't. He's evil, Ruth. Evil from the time he came from your womb.

Foul he is, with the devil in him. He must suffer to be made right, just as Jesus suffered."

More feeble pleading from his mother, more screams from his own throat... and then he wasn't enclosed anymore. It was not his father or his mother reaching down to him, but Clure Daugherty.

"Jason, what's wrong with you?" Daugherty said, extending his hand. "You were screaming nonsense."

Lybrand grasped Daugherty's hand and scrambled out of the shed. He fell on his knees, gasping like he had been choked.

"You were yelling like I was your daddy," Daugherty said. The big man, the fighting spirit now out of him, thought about that a moment and chuckled. "You called me 'Papa'!"

Lybrand rose to his feet. After a few moments he was more his old self again, though blanched.

"You just forget what happened here," he said. "Concentrate on staying clear of Orv Brown. Get up to the Molly Bee and stay in the cabin."

"I can't spend all my time twiddling my thumbs up there, Jason. A man's got to come to town for a drink or a bite to eat."

"Look, I don't care what you do. Just stay away from Orv Brown, and lay low. You ruin the plan, you'll be held responsible."

"Same goes for you, Jason."

Lybrand wheeled and stalked away.

Abel Patterson watched the boy, as he often did, and wondered if there was a force that brought people together, or if they just met by chance, like leaves falling atop one another in the forest. Patterson had never expected to become guardian of a boy—especially not in the manner he had become unofficial guardian of this one.

The boy was seated in a chair, looking at pictures in a secondhand book Patterson had bought today. It was a depressing little volume featuring woodcuts showing the souls of dead children being lifted from coffins by winged angels, and Jesus smiling down from above the clouds at young orphans beside fresh graves marked MOTHER and FATHER, but Patterson hadn't been able to find anything better. Snow Sky opened a new business a day, folks said, but so far few people were selling books.

Patterson walked across the rented room and touched the boy's shoulder. "Spencer, you ready for sleeping now?"

The boy put down the book, stood, and walked to his bed. Silently he undressed and crawled in. He pulled the covers to his chin.

You sure don't have much to say, do you, boy? Patterson wanted to comment. But it would have been pointless, for he had said it a score of times before, and it had never drawn response. In the time he had cared for young Spencer Vestal, he doubted the boy had said enough words to fill one page of that book he had been reading. Given the circumstances in which the two had been thrown together, it didn't seem that should bother Patterson, but it did.

"Good night, Spence," he said. The boy said his own good night—just a faint, quick whisper—and turned his face toward the wall. In a minute or less he began the slow, steady breathing of sleep.

Patterson went to his chair and sank into it, feeling terribly depressed. He was depressed a lot these days, and in a way that made no sense, for he had always figured that if he had money he would be happy, and he had more of it now than he had ever thought he would. He somewhat regretted having put it in the bank, for banked money could be traced much more easily, but he had not felt comfortable with the idea of keeping all that cash in hand. In Snow Sky it would promptly be stolen.

Snow Sky. Here at last in the town that he had hoped would solve his problem, only to find it had not. The sister he had sought was not here, contrary to what he had expected, and no one seemed to know anything about her. Much distance in miles and years stood between his sister and him. Maybe it was just as well he had not found her, for she might have refused to take Spencer off his hands anyway.

Which would have left Patterson in the same predicament: playing guardian to a boy he had not asked for, and whose nearly unbroken silence disturbed Patterson almost as much as the ugly scars on the young white body. What had this boy gone through so far in life? Was it past suffering that kept him silent?

Patterson stretched, shook himself like a wet dog. He had to get out. He couldn't sit here lost in dark thoughts. He rose and picked up his hat. Fingering it, he went to the boy's bed.

"I'm going out for a while," he said, in case the boy was awake enough to hear. "I'll be back soon. You just sleep. I'll leave the lamp burning."

The boy did not respond. He seemed still to be asleep. Patterson put on his hat and walked out the door, wondering why this child could so break his heart.

When Patterson clicked the door shut behind him, Spencer sat up and looked around the empty room. He thought briefly about secretly following his guardian, as he had other times, but tonight he decided not to. He was content to simply stay where he was and think about the man whom Abel Patterson had accosted outside the dance hall. The man from the inn—the man who talked about the woman who worried about the welfare of little boys.

Spencer lay back, his hands behind his head, basking in the knowledge that somewhere, at least, one person cared about him, It was a new feeling for him . . . a good one. He smiled at the ceiling.

Cochran had been unable to find Abel Patterson, which did not surprise him, but did worry him. He had already come to think of Patterson's detective skills as Frogg's only hope. Right now Cochran could use a few detective skills himself. But inwardly he wondered if he really would have the courage to approach for help the same man who had roughed him up and threatened him only a day ago.

Still, Frogg had to be cleared, and Cochran had no idea how to do that alone. He was tired now at the end of the day, and ready to give up, but for Frogg's sake he decided to look around a bit longer, poking through a few more saloons and dance halls in hope of spotting the former Pinkerton man.

"Howdy."

Cochran wheeled, drawing in his breath. Lord, but he was tense—jumpy as a cricket in a stove. He was sure that Earl Cobb had noticed that, too; he was standing only six feet away, cleaning his nails with a pocketknife.

"Hello, Marshal," Cochran said, recovering. "You surprised me."

"Thought you looked a bit startled. Sorry. Just trying to be sociable."

Cochran doubted that. This peace officer didn't seem the sort to make idle small talk.

There followed a time of silence that sat uneasily with Cochran but didn't seem to at all affect the marshal, who calmly kept digging dirt from beneath his nails and wiping it on his trousers.

"Still got your friend sitting in the jail," Cobb remarked casually.

"He isn't my friend—I met him riding into town. Remember?"

"Pardon me. I forgot. Anyway, I still got him in jail. But it's a funny thing: I don't really think he killed that Viola fellow. Ain't sure why. You ever get notions like that that you can't quite explain?"

Cochran was so surprised he didn't know what to say.

Cobb continued. "My main problem is, I don't have any good evidence in Frogg's favor—and Frogg did have that Bible on him."

Another long, uncomfortable pause. Cochran wondered if he was about to be arrested. He asked, "Is there anything specific you need of me, Marshal?"

"Need? No. Just passing the time. Things get slow in the law business; you have time to do that. What business are you in, Mr. Cochran?"

"I'm an innkeeper."

"Is that right? Where?"

"About a day and a half's ride up the road yonder. The Cochran Inn."

Cobb nodded. "Heard of it." Then he looked thoughtful. "So that means that Frogg and maybe even Viola would have come by your inn."

Cochran hesitantly decided to risk giving the marshal one piece of truth. "Frogg I didn't see, but Viola stayed at my inn. It took me some time to realize the man who was killed was him."

Cobb didn't believe that; a name such as Viola is remembered. He didn't challenge Cochran, however.

"Did you talk to Viola while he was there?"

"Some."

"What did he say about his trip to Snow Sky?"

"Not much. Just that he had an unpleasant job ahead and dreaded it."

"What kind of unpleasant job?"

"A meeting with someone, I think. He didn't say more and I didn't ask. Does it matter?"

Cobb folded and pocketed his knife. "Maybe not, maybe so. I was just hoping you'd be able to provide something more to help me. Thanks, and sorry for the bother."

"No bother at all, Marshal."

Cochran walked away, wondering what this encounter had been all about. The marshal's word that he thought Frogg innocent was a profound and pleasing shock—if it had been sincere. Cochran couldn't tell; Earl Cobb seemed a fox-smart peace officer, the kind to pick his way along without revealing exactly where he was going, or how much you had unwittingly helped him along the way. Cochran entered a saloon, mostly to get out of Cobb's sight and think over what had just transpired.

For his part, Cobb had some thinking over to do, too, for Tudor Cochran had just given him an interesting piece of information: P. D. Viola had been fearing a coming meeting in Snow Sky. With whom? Lybrand? But that made no sense if all Viola was coming to do was to help establish a church. Why should a preacher dread that, given that such was his life's business? Once again the pieces didn't fit.

Cobb considered the possibility that the innkeeper himself was lying about it all. Maybe Cochran himself had killed Viola. Perhaps some grudge had developed while Viola stayed at his inn. Maybe he suspected the preacher carried a lot of money.

But Cobb didn't buy that. He could tell by instinct that Cochran was not the killing type. He seemed the sort who would dodge a bug instead of step on it.

Yet Cochran was covering up something, Cobb suspected. Probably about his knowledge of Hiram Frogg; Cobb found it difficult to believe the two men really knew each other as minimally as they claimed. He glanced down the street, wondering where Cochran might have gone. He caught a glimpse of the innkeeper just as Cochran entered the door of the Eagle Wing Saloon.

Patterson sat alone at a back table, sipping whiskey. A shadow fell across his table and he looked up. The innkeeper he had attacked outside the dance hall stood there, looking nervously at him.

"Hello," Cochran said. He was holding his hat tightly, rolling and unrolling the edge of the brim. Ironic, Cochran was thinking, that he should chance upon Patterson in the very saloon he had entered to get away from Earl Cobb and his questions.

Patterson shook his head and looked back down at his whiskey. "What do you want? You still trying to poke into my affairs?"

"Please. I'd like to ask you to hear me out about something. My name is Tudor Cochran, in case I never told you." He put out his hand.

Patterson ignored it and looked away.

Cochran lowered his hand and said, "This will just take a moment or two. May I sit down?"

Patterson was not pleased by the request, but waved curtly toward the other chair at his table. Cochran quickly pulled it back and sat down in it, so obviously tense he looked like he would be triggered to the ceiling if anyone around so much as stomped a foot too loudly. Patterson took another sip of his whiskey and glowered coldly at Cochran, thinking of how the man reminded him of a thoroughly unwelcome stray dog who had wandered into his yard and refused to leave.

"Well?" Patterson prompted gruffly.

"I need your help," Cochran said, leaning forward a little, still rolling his hat brim in his lap.

"Help?" That struck Patterson so funny that he laughed aloud. "Why should I help you with anything?"

"Because you're probably the only man in Snow Sky with the ability to clear the name of an innocent man being wrongly suspected of a killing."

Patterson frowned. Those words implied rather uncomfortably that Cochran knew something about his identity and professional background. "What are you getting at?"

"I suppose I'm trying to offer you a job."

Patterson frowned, then laughed again. "A job! What makes you think I need one?"

"I suppose you don't. But an innocent man could be imprisoned, or worse, if you don't agree to help me clear him."

Patterson had to admit that this was becoming interesting. "All right, friend, you've got my ear. This is just loco enough to rouse my curiosity."

"Mr. Patterson, I want you to—"

"Why did you call me that?"

"Well, it's your name, isn't it? Abel Patterson?"

Concern bolted through Patterson, who had thought no one in Snow Sky knew his identity. "My name is Johnson," he asserted strongly. "Where did you hear different?"

Cochran's mouth went dry, and he realized he had made a slip. He should have known Patterson would be concerned when he found out his real name was known. Cochran felt his opportunity slipping away, yet he knew he couldn't reveal where he had gotten his information. If Patterson knew a newspaperman had been talking about him, he would be out of town within the hour. So Cochran blurted, "I used to live in Chicago. I read about you in the papers. You were pointed out to me once. I knew you looked familiar when I saw you at the inn, but I didn't recall who you were until a couple of hours ago." Cochran spilled out the lie, then hoped Patterson would not challenge it, for Cochran had never been to Chicago and knew nothing about the city.

Patterson didn't question Cochran. His mind was occupied with only one thought: He now must leave Snow Sky. Clean his money out of the bank and take off. If someone here knew him, he couldn't afford to linger. But leaving would be troublesome. Could he endure weeks of aimless riding with the responsibility of young Spencer Vestal heavy on his shoulders?

"I'm not trying to cause you worry," Cochran continued. "All I want is your help. You are a fine criminal investigator, or so I was told."

"And you're a man who's followed me for miles and poked his nose in where it doesn't belong."

"I don't deny it. I did that for my wife. But this is a different matter. This is for my friend, and it could be life or death. His."

Patterson drained off his whiskey. "So what are you asking?"

Cochran leaned over a bit more so he could further lower his voice. "You heard of the killing of a preacher named Viola?"

"I did. Why is that your concern?"

"Because the best friend I've got is in the jail, suspected of the murder. He and I have both told the law here that we don't know each other, so I've just now put my safety into your hands."

"Is your friend guilty?"

"No."

"How do you know?"

"Because I was with him all the way into Snow Sky and a little while after that. And even if I hadn't been I would know Hiram didn't do it. He's rough, but no murderer."

"So why not go to the law and tell them what you know?"

"They wouldn't believe me, and likely I'd just become another suspect. And there's some evidence against Hiram." He told about finding the New Testament and how it had figured into the situation.

Patterson turned his empty shot glass between his fingers, shook his head. "I see no reason for me to get involved in a murder investigation. I don't need money and I don't want the attention, and it isn't my affair. I'm a former detective, not an active one."

Cochran's heart sank. He said, "Surely there is something I can offer you that would make you change your mind."

"Not a thing."

Cochran sank back in his chair. "Then there's not much I can do for Hiram."

"That's your concern, not mine. I got my own concern, and it's more than enough for me."

Interpreting him, Cochran asked, "The boy?"

Patterson said nothing, lifting his glass to let a final drop fall from its rim onto his tongue.

Cochran asked something else that was on his mind. "Mr. Patterson, if you'll do nothing for Hiram Frogg, at least do something for my wife. Give me some word to take back to her about the boy. Who is he? Does she have cause to worry for him?"

Patterson looked at Cochran in silence, not sure he

should say anything. Finally he did. "His name is
Spencer Vestal. He's a young fellow whose path crossed
mine. He's in need of a home. I came here to find him
one, but that hasn't worked out."

And at that a new and surprising thought flew like
a comet through Cochran's mind—a frightening, probably foolish, but wonderfully possible option. Ideally, it
was the sort of thing a man should talk about for months
and talk over with his wife, but at the moment Cochran
had neither months nor wife available. In less than five
seconds he made his decision and presented his propo-
sition to Patterson. "Mr. Patterson, if you will help me,
then I'll help you in turn. I'll give that boy a home with
my wife and me."

Patterson stared at Cochran, then down at the
tabletop. Cochran leaned forward again, pressing his
offer. "All I ask is that you help me find who really
killed that preacher, or at the very least show it wasn't
Frogg who did it. Do that, and the boy will become my
responsibility."

A home for Spencer was just what Patterson had
been looking for, but now that he had found one he was
unsure what to do.

"Well? Will you do it?" Cochran prodded.

Patterson stood suddenly, dug money from his
pocket, dropped it on the table, and stalked out. Cochran
watched him go, then sank back in his seat, more
dejected than ever.

Chapter 8

―――――――◆―◆―――――――

The Following Evening

Jason Lybrand awakened with a yell, the dream image of his father's face still clearly before him. Or had it been the face of Viola? Or both—dreams could sometimes twist reality in impossible ways.

Lybrand, who had fallen asleep at his supper table with a copy of the *Argus* before him, put his face into his hands and rubbed his eyes. Got to get in control again, he thought. Can't let myself panic.

He picked up the newspaper and reread Oliver Byers' coverage of the death of Viola, and of the continuing official suspicions that Hiram Frogg was the killer. The story should have made Lybrand feel safe and confident. It didn't. He wadded the paper and threw it into his cold fireplace.

The more time that went by, the more uncertain and threatened Lybrand felt. He had a bitter feeling that bad things were coming; there would by a payday, and he would be on the short end.

He stood. Get a grip on yourself, man, he thought. Things really aren't so bad, no matter how you feel.

He reminded himself of the several matters going in his favor—particularly the suspect already jailed in connection with Viola's murder. And even without such a convenient scapegoat, why should anyone have cause to think the fine young preacher at Snow Sky's House of Prayer would be a killer? He had never given the community reason to distrust him.

Lybrand knew he was a good actor; he had put on many performances under many names through the years, sometimes professionally on stage, sometimes off it. The world of theatrics and make-believe had attracted him as far back as he could remember. In that world an abused city boy could escape the tyranny of an insane father. Lybrand had always felt it ironic that on stage, where every action and word was predetermined and the final climax settled even before the opening line was spoken, he felt more free than anywhere else. The fictional life of the stage was more true and authentic to Lybrand than the cruel real one he lived in.

But being an actor had one drawback: it paid very little. Lybrand thus found himself beginning to use his acting skills in innovative, self-profiting ways. By portraying a down-on-his-luck traveler, he found he could snare a contribution from a church. As a just-discharged, jobless soldier, he could talk his way into a free meal. And as a street-corner preacher, imitating the religious rantings of his obsessed rum-addicted father, he could talk spiritual fervor into the heart of—and money out of the pocket of—the sort of folk who were ready to believe anything that gave them hope and a sense of importance.

Eventually Lybrand had begun calling himself "Reverend" and taking on his preacher persona almost full-time. It had its disadvantages—womanizing, drinking, gambling, and the like had to be done on the sneak—but it was also lucrative.

He involved himself in less sophisticated crimes as well, sometimes participating in robberies, burglaries, and even rapes, with his two old backstreet cronies, Dade and Daugherty. But Lybrand disliked crude crimes; he preferred a smooth swindle to a back-alley pocket-cleaning. As time went by he concentrated most of his attention on his lucrative clergyman persona.

No one except the late P. D. Viola had ever come close to exposing Lybrand—and that had almost happened only because Lybrand let his passions for Viola's daughter make him careless.

P. D. Viola. The man's very name roused Lybrand's disgust. Yet Viola had been useful to him once. Lybrand had successfully deceived Viola and his family for quite some time—so thoroughly that he had gained the secret intimacy of Viola's lovely daughter, Francine. The memory of her stirred Lybrand's blood. Beautiful, passionate she had been. The fifth in a string of wives for Lybrand, who married but never bothered with the legal messiness of divorce, which was troublesome and, in Lybrand's view, unnecessary. In Francine's case it truly had proven unnecessary, for she had died giving birth to the stillborn child Lybrand had planted in her well before their marriage, bitterly shaming her pious father.

Lybrand thought back wistfully on Francine, then tossed aside her memory like outdated correspondence. She was dead, that was that, and he would have to content himself with the charms of other women. Dutch Polly had hardly been a fit replacement for Francine, but she had served her limited purpose well for a time.

But now Polly was making threats that had him worried. He had been foolish to allow a crib girl to fall in love with him. His own brother years ago had made such a mistake, and had died in his own bed as a result, stabbed by the prostitute who had wanted from him that which he would not give.

Lybrand was only just now realizing that Polly was equally dangerous to him. If she told others of his dallyings with her, that would be the end of the Reverend Jason Lybrand in Snow Sky. Perhaps Daugherty had been right. Perhaps he had been a fool to talk so much to Polly. Yet it had seemed harmless; the woman was so opium-dulled that she had not seemed even to hear half of what he said to her. Now he was sure she had in fact heard him, and understood much more than he had guessed.

He had been fretting over the situation all day, remaining locked away in his cabin. Something would have to be done. Otherwise things might turn sour.

He rose and walked to the window of his cabin. The sky was dull and gray; a change in the weather was coming. Well, let it come. He had to start preparing a sermon for Sunday morning in any case. Perhaps something on the need for the church in civilized society, its role in bringing peace and welfare to the frontier, so on and so on. Something to make his churchmen feel important, righteous—and to heighten their sense of Christian generosity when the offering plate came around.

Lybrand went to his table and sat down, thumbing through his Bible for appropriate verses. Ironically, the first thing he found was a reference to the Whore of Babylon, which put him in mind again of Dutch Polly and her threats. He slammed the Bible shut and paced around the room, wishing he was free to walk down to a saloon and get thoroughly drunk. Again he despised being tied to a public image of saintliness.

He returned to the window. The wind was up. Lybrand scanned the heavens and then dropped his gaze. To his surprise, it came to rest on Earl Cobb, who was standing leaned against a fence just down the road. He was shaving off a piece of wood with his knife. Lybrand had the peculiar and unsettling feeling the marshal was watching his house. His paranoid sense of doom surged like an ocean breaker.

Lybrand let the curtain fall and turned away.

Patterson watched Spencer sleep and mused over the unexpected offer Cochran had made, and the inexplicable reluctance he felt to accept it. At last a chance was at hand to be free of this tag-along boy, but now he didn't want to be. Patterson could make no sense of his own feelings.

Patterson and Spencer had shared a strange companionship; but then, it had begun after a strange meeting.

Spencer had come into Patterson's life—or more precisely, he had come into Spencer's—in a small valley several miles from Denver. His Pinkerton days behind him, Patterson had been making his living doing menial detective and guard jobs, and had become involved in the most menial yet: delivery of extortion money from a wealthy Denver banking baron to some human maggot holed up in the mountains. What sin the extortioner held over the head of the rich man Patterson neither knew nor cared to know—but it must have been significant, for the banker had readily parted with fifty thousand dollars to keep his tormentor quiet. He had hired Patterson to carry the cash because he knew of Patterson's reputation with the Pinkertons, and felt he would be both honest enough and capable enough to safely make the delivery.

Patterson had ridden with the cash in his saddlebags, following the crude map the extortioner had provided, and all the way had fought an inner battle. Why not take the money for himself? Let the rich man's secrets catch up with him—that wasn't Patterson's worry. Likely the man deserved to be extorted and discredited.

But Patterson had not yielded. In the end he found himself riding the final stretch of mountain trail leading to the place where the extortioner was to receive the cash.

At the end of that trail Patterson had found a tiny cabin in a clearing, and outside it, a boy of about eleven very hard at work with a shovel.

He was digging a grave. For the extortioner, it appeared; a fat man's corpse lay stretched out beside the shallow hole. The body matched the description Patterson had been given of the extortioner.

The boy silently watched Patterson's approach. Leaning on his shovel, he said nothing, but stared as sweat dripped off his brow and soaked through his shirt.

Patterson gestured toward the corpse. "Your father?"
The boy nodded.

"What's your name?"

No answer. It would be days before the boy answered that question. By that time Patterson would have come to understand, through the scars and the eternal, veiled fear in the young eyes, that life had been terribly hard for Spencer Vestal, and that the greatest mercy it had yet shown him was the stopping of the heart of the father who beat his son more than he spoke to him.

From what Patterson could tell, the extortioner had died naturally. Heart, probably. Patterson had seen plenty of death in his time, and knew men of this one's girth had a way of just dropping dead as a run-down clock once their hearts wearied of their task.

"Would you like me to help you bury him?" Patterson had asked the silent boy.

Still unspeaking, Spencer had offered him the shovel. Patterson finished the grave and laid the obese corpse in it, then began shoveling dirt atop him before he realized such a thing might be difficult for the boy to see.

"You want to go somewhere else while I cover him?" Patterson had asked. But Spencer had simply shaken his head and stayed at the graveside, masking any emotion he might have felt. Later, when Patterson would see the boy's scars, he would speculate that the hidden emotion might have been relief.

When the grave was filled, Patterson had leaned on the shovel and considered what to do. Without making a conscious decision, he nonetheless had concluded already that he would not return the extortion payment. His life had made a moral downhill slide for months now, and he simply let himself slide a little farther—and it was surprisingly easy. The old banker surely had plenty more money. Probably much of it ill-gotten, too, judging from the fact he obviously was open to extortion.

Patterson had climbed back into his saddle before he had realized that the boy couldn't simply be abandoned. But what could he, an odd-job drifter with saddlebags full of stolen payoff money, do with a scruffy kid in tow? He couldn't take the boy to the law, or to an orphanage, for someone would ask how Patterson had managed to get him. Even if he lied, they surely would ask the boy, too—and if the lad ever found his tongue, he might just tell about the man who came to bring his father's extortion payment, then decided to keep it.

And that was how Abel Patterson came to be the guardian, against his will and the boy's, of Spencer Vestal.

Patterson had known he would have to find the boy a home—but how? It would have to be with someone who would accept the boy with no questions and no intention of involving the law. In a flash it had come to him: his sister. Living now, last he had heard, with her husband in the mining camp of Snow Sky, Colorado. Even though he had never kept up with his sister as well as he should have, maybe she still would take the boy, give him a home, see to him without getting Patterson himself involved or in trouble. It was the only option he could think of.

Patterson had taken the extortioner's horse for the boy, and man and boy had left immediately for Snow Sky, Patterson as tense as if he had a wasp down his pants, but also excited. He had money now, more than he knew what to do with—and soon he might be rid of the boy. He would have the rest of his days to use that money to buy a new life in which he could forget the old one and its one unforgivable failure—the time he had failed to be there to save his brother from a robber's bullet on a dark Chicago street. Though he had tried at least a hundred times to convince himself his feeling of responsibility for Roland's death was irrational, he had not succeeded. A sense of failure and guilt had continued to haunt Patterson, led him to liquor, ended his career with the Pinkertons, and left him doing jobs as low as delivering—and now stealing—extortion money.

Spencer moved in his bed now and opened his eyes. He saw Patterson looking down at him, and for a moment fear flashed through him. Patterson saw it. It saddened him.

He reached out and touched Spencer's forehead. "You sleeping all right?" he asked.

The boy nodded.

"I've been doing some thinking," Patterson said, hardly able to believe he was about to say what he was. "I was wondering if maybe you might like to stay with me. Let me be your father. I don't know much about boys beyond that I was one myself once—but I can learn. I can give you a good life, better than any you had before. There's enough money for it. Maybe someday there might even be a woman who can be your mother."

Spencer rolled away, turning his back on Patterson. There already is a woman who could be my mother, he was thinking. She's back at that inn, and I know she cares for me because I heard her husband say so. That's who I want, not you.

He said none of it, but Patterson sensed the rejection. He stood and walked over to his own bed, lay down, and stared at the ceiling.

All right, he thought. Innkeeper Cochran, I'll take your offer. I'll try to help your friend, and you can have the boy.

Even though now I don't want to give him up.

The Next Morning

The marshal's office door burst open with a bang, awakening Cobb from a good sleep that was no more than an hour and a half old. A razor of a voice sliced into his eardrums. Then another voice moaned—or maybe it was a floorboard creaking. Got to find some other place to live besides this blasted office, Cobb thought as he rolled over. Lousy slamming doors, yelling prisoners, creaking floors, belching deputies—won't let a man sleep. . . .

Suddenly he was being shaken. Blearily he opened his eyes. Cap Corley said, "Earl, I'm sorry to stir you out of there, but we got trouble."

Cobb sat up, his skull full of cobwebs. "What is it?"

"Orv Brown just got himself shot."

Without a word Cobb rose and pulled on his clothing.

Another moan came from the office. Cobb threw back the curtain, walked around the corner, and saw Brown lying on the floor with blood on his side. A couple of men Cobb didn't know were kneeling beside Brown.

"Orv, what the devil have you gone and done?"

"His name was Clure Daugherty," Orv said.

"Who?"

"The one who just shot me, dang it! He shot me and run, and folks leaned over me and said that was Clure Daugherty who done it and it was good that he wasn't drunk because he likely would have killed me then. Oh . . . Lord have mercy, my side's throbbing!"

Cobb knelt and examined the wound. "It don't look all that bad, Orv." To the other men there, he said, "Who are you?"

They told their names, which meant nothing to Cobb. "We seen it happen," the one with the sharp-edged voice said.

"Why didn't you take him to get patched up?"

"We're new in Snow Sky. We don't know how to find no doctor. Besides, he said he wanted to come here first thing, so we brought him."

Orv had pushed himself up onto his rump and was looking at his bloody side. "I think you're right, Earl. Didn't punch too bad a hole." He paused. "The worst of it is that Kimmie's going to kill me. She's been harping on me already for looking for those robbers, saying I'd get myself hurt."

"Smart woman, then," Cobb said. "Smarter than her husband. Dang, Orv, why'd you come here instead of going to get patched?"

"Why do you think? I want you to go after him before the trail gets cold."

"I figured as much." Cobb stood, sighing. He

could imagine his snug bed beckoning silently, seductively to him back in his room. But there would be no more sleeping now.

"You do anything to prompt this bullet, Orv?"

One of the other men spoke up. "I can vouch he didn't do nothing but ask the big fellow why he robbed him. The man just up and pulled a pistol, and blam, there was this one on the floor a-bleeding. Then the big one took off on a run. A littler fellow rose up at the faro table and lit out after him. I thought he was chasing him at first, but then they took off together."

"How am I supposed to find this Daugherty?"

"Somebody said in the saloon that Daugherty has been holed up somewhere up at the Molly Bee Pass with somebody. Probably that runt from the faro table."

"Ready to ride, Earl?" Cap Corley asked, spreading his white mustache as he drew his mouth into a thin line.

"Ready as I'll ever be."

They gathered guns, ammunition, jackets, hats. "Orv, get over to Walt Chambers, get yourself patched up, and go home to Kimmie, and next time somebody robs you just leave the responding to the law, you hear?"

Orv's only answer was a groan. Cobb slammed the door as he left. Within ten minutes he and Corley were out of town, riding up the trail toward the Molly Bee Pass. Above them rolled thick clouds, heavy with the promise of rain and lightning.

Cobb reined to a halt beneath an outcrop of rock. He looked around.

"What is it, Earl?"

"I don't know. Just a bad feeling."

"Yeah. I've had the same one for the last ten minutes."

Cobb didn't like to hear that. Cap Corley was an old Texas Ranger who had come through many an ambush by both Indians and Mexican bandits, and his instincts were honed like a keen blade. Cobb trusted his own instincts, Corley's even more. When their intuitions spoke as one, they were worth listening to.

"If this Daugherty hadn't shot Orv I might be tempted to let him go," Cobb admitted.

"But he did shoot him," Corley reminded him.

"So he did." Cobb sighed. "Come on, then—but be careful."

They proceeded. The land tilted up, and rock formations contorted into weird sculptures by centuries of rain and wind thrust up on either side of them. Both men kept their eyes and ears tuned for any hint of ambush.

"Most likely they're on across the mountain by now, Earl," Corley said.

"Maybe. Or maybe they're holed up at Apex McCall's old place. I hear from the mountain prospectors that there's been somebody there lately."

As thunder rumbled overhead, Cobb and Corley made it through the rocks without incident, and when they came out on the other side they were on a wide, smooth level that ended abruptly in a wide gorge. Into the gorge spilled Silver Falls, which was merely a trickle in summer and fall and frozen in winter, but which now was a sizable waterfall, engorged with spring runoff.

The gorge was a big eroded gully about thirty feet deep, filled with rock and fallen timber that had been pulled in by water or gravity. On the other side of it was a mazelike rock tangle, and beyond that the cabin of the late hermit prospector Apex McCall, who had died the previous winter. His cabin had sat empty since—except for lately, as Cobb had been told.

It was a guess at best that Orv Brown's assailant was living at the McCall cabin, but the closer Cobb got, the more he believed that in fact was the case. At several points along the trail he and Corley had seen fresh tracks of two hard-pushed horses.

When they reached the edge of the gorge Cobb and Corley dismounted. Before them stretched a rickety bridge made of logs and puncheons—a crude, very unstable structure built last summer by McCall and several other prospectors who had worked up around the Molly Bee. Their prospecting had not come to much, and by winter all but McCall had abandoned the Molly Bee. The bridge, flimsy though it was, remained in use, though, for the Molly Bee Pass provided one more route into and out of Snow Sky—though a rugged one.

For a long time Cobb and Corley stood quietly, letting their horses rest while they listened for any warning sounds. The crashing waterfall, thunder, and rising winds were all they could hear.

"Suppose we'd better cross," Cobb said.

"Yeah."

Cobb led his horse toward the bridge, but stopped. That same intuitive sense of danger was ringing an alarm in his brain. He looked at Corley and saw something in the weathered face that might have been fear—if the old Texas Ranger was capable of such.

"What do you think, Cap?"

Corley bit his mustache. "That there'll be trouble—but I ain't run from trouble yet."

Cobb nodded, took a breath, and started across the bridge.

The narrow bridge was about fifteen feet long, but seemed twice that long by the time Cobb reached its center. The sagging logs and puncheons creaked and snapped beneath the weight of him and his horse. Cobb's eyes swept the rocks ahead, looking for movement that might indicate ambush.

He had just neared the end of the bridge when Corley led his own mount out onto it. Halfway across, the older man stopped, his eyes narrowing, flashing. Cobb turned in time to see Corley reaching for his saddle rifle, and right then a shot cracked somewhere high in the rocks ahead, and Corley's horse shuddered, spasmed, and fell forward. The old ranger was pinned between the horse and the log rail of the bridge.

"Cap!" Cobb screamed. He dropped his own horse's reins, slid out his rifle, and headed toward his trapped partner.

He was almost to Corley when another shot blasted, Corley's forehead shattered, and the straining bridge rail broke. Corley's body pitched downward, making a full turn in the air before hitting the rocks and the gushing water below. The dead horse fell next, landing directly atop Corley's body, and then both man and horse washed on down and out of sight in the tangle of logs, rock, and muddy runoff below. Cobb's own horse trumpeted in terror and bolted on into the rocks. Cobb saw it no more.

"Cap!" Cobb screamed again, uselessly. Then the unseen gunman in the rocks spat another slug from his rifle, the wind of it fanning Cobb's face. Cobb stepped back, tripped, teetered with his stomach leaping to his throat, then fell off the side of the bridge as a magnificent cannonblast of thunder roared from horizon to horizon.

Chapter 9

Below in Snow Sky, Oliver Byers lifted his head to listen to that same rumble of thunder, and at the same moment heard a knock on his office door. He rubbed his face, which was covered with stiff whiskers, for he had been up both late last night and early this morning, poring over an anxiously awaited packet of information that finally had arrived in the mail. Byers loved his sleep; he did not sacrifice it for much, even for journalism. But what was in this packet had been fascinating enough to make him do so.

He folded his papers together and put them back into the packet, glancing quickly at the last thing to go in: a portrait of Jason Lybrand, actor, dressed as the fur-hatted Col. Nimrod Wildfire in a backstreet Chicago production of *The Lion of the West*.

At Byers' door was a boy with thick blond hair that hung to his shoulders. He was dressed in tatters. Byers recognized him as a son of one of the local prostitutes.

The smell of the unwashed young fellow made the newspaperman wrinkle his nose.

"I got something for you," the boy said, holding up a note.

"For me?"

"That's what I said."

Smart-tongued little squat, Byers thought, taking the note. "Who's it from?" he asked.

"Dutch Polly from the cribs. You going to pay me for that or not?"

Byers fished out a coin. "Now take your money and get away from here before you stink up the place," Byers said. He closed the door.

Lousy harlot's brood. Byers hated the sort. Snow Sky had more than its share of such cast-off humans, many of them old even before they were grown. Byers often wondered where the beggars, thieves, prostitutes, and gamblers of mining and cattle towns came from, and what made them what they were. It was a question that piqued his journalistic curiosity. At one time it might have also piqued his human sympathy, but years of treating people increasingly as journalistic specimens and subjects for stories and less as human beings had greatly reduced Byers' capacity for caring. When he had first noticed that numbing process beginning he had worried about it, but time finally had taken care of that, too.

He opened the note. In crude, big letters, it said:

Mister news paper, I can tell you abot the precher Jason Librann and the way he lays with harlits and cheets the peple in his church

if you will com see me. I am Polly Coots who
thay call Dutch Polly.

Byers read and reread the note, hardly believing
he had received it at such an ironically appropriate
time. He had just spent a full night learning some
damning facts about the supposed Reverend Lybrand—
and now a local prostitute was ready to give him even
more information.

Byers smiled, folded Dutch Polly's note, went back
to his desk, and put the note into the packet. He closed
and tied the packet, then looked around his office for a
secure place to hide it. Nothing seemed to do. Finally
he simply stuck it into a filing cabinet. He blew out the
lights, put on his derby, and walked to his little house
up the hill behind the *Argus* office, planning to shave
and clean up before he met Polly Coots—and then he
stopped, realizing how silly that was. Dutch Polly probably hadn't had a man clean up for her in years. He
turned on his heel.

Entering the street, he headed for the southeast
portion of Snow Sky, where the cribs stood. It was not an
area much frequented by him, except when he was there
to gather facts about one more shooting or stabbing. Byers
loved vice in others because it generated good news copy,
but personally he shunned it—not out of moral fortitude,
but because a man could hardly keep up a schedule of sin
and mining town journalism at the same time.

Byers reached the cribs, which stood in a row
along Scofield Street's south side. Their purpose was

Track Down And Capture Exciting Western Adventure!
WANTED!
LOUIS L'AMOUR COLLECTION!
REWARD OFFERED
Mail your "WANTED" poster today. (see inside)
Make your "wanted" claim and receive your rightful reward!
• A free authentic Louis L'Amour calendar!
• A free preview of the bestselling SACKETT
And much more...

FREE — MAGNIFICENT WALL CALENDAR!
FREE — PREVIEW OF SACKETT
- No Obligation!   • No Purchase Necessary!

"WANTED!"
STICKER
GOES HERE

Yes! I'm claiming my reward!

Send SACKETT for 15 days free! If I keep this volume, I will pay just $10.95 plus shipping and handling. Future Louis L'Amour Westerns will be sent to me about once a month, on a 15-day, Free-Examination basis. I understand that there is no minimum number of books to buy, and I may cancel my subscription at any time. The Free Louis L'Amour wall calendar is mine to keep even if I decide to return SACKETT.

NAME _____

ADDRESS _____

CITY _____

STATE _____ ZIP _____

MY NO RISK GUARANTEE:

There's no obligation to buy. The free calendar is mine to keep. I may preview SACKETT and any other Louis L'Amour book for 15 days. If I don't want it, I simply return the book and owe nothing. If I keep it, I pay only $10.95 (plus postage and handling).

70136

IL23

Track down and capture exciting western adventure from one of America's foremost novelists!

• It's free! • No obligation! • Exclusive value!

made blatant by the sign above the crib row—SALLY'S
PARADISE ROW—and the smaller signs naming the individual crib occupants. The latter were tacked onto the
small, windowed gablelike protrusions beside each
crib. Byers walked down the row, reading—JESSICA,
KATHLEEN, SALLY RUTH, JEZEBEL . . . and at last, DUTCH
POLLY.

Byers took off his derby and knocked on the door.
He heard an answering shuffle inside, then fumbling at
the latch, and the crib door swung open.

Byers fought off an impulse to recoil. Dutch Polly,
in the diffused light inside the doorway, was a discon-
certing mix of youth and age. She surely was no more
than thirty and just as surely no less than fifty. She
reeked of gin.

"You that newspaper man?" she asked after she had
looked him over.

"I am. Oliver Byers."

She hiked up the shoulder of her dress, which had
been pulled low. "Come on in," she said.

He stepped inside. He was hard-pressed to breathe
in the cramped, unventilated little room. The crib
reeked of spilled liquor, crushed-out cigars, sweat, un-
clean flesh. On a shelf sat a new bottle of gin and a
half-empty quart bottle of laudanum. Dutch Polly, obviously, was addicted to the only type of escape available
to most crib girls. In many cases it was the final escape
they turned to when living wasn't worth it anymore.
Looking at Dutch Polly, Byers could only wonder how
long it would be until she made that ultimate decision.

"Sit down," Polly said, waving at a chair. She
picked up the bottle of gin and poured some into a

greasy glass on her bedside table. "Want some?" she asked.

"No, no," Byers said. "Too early for me."

Polly took a long swallow. "The earlier the better, I always say." When the glass was empty, she poured it full again. "I didn't know if you would come."

"I was intrigued by your note," Byers said. "I happen to be quite interested in Lybrand."

"You ain't in his church, are you?"

"No. I'm not a churchgoing man. And I don't trust Lybrand."

Her breath was strong with alcohol. "You're smart, then. He's bad. I know how bad he is. Stands in that pulpit and tells people to be good and takes their money and then does every bad thing he tells them not to. Even with the likes of me."

"Why are you telling me about this?" he asked.

"So you could put him in the paper for what he is."

"You hate him that much?"

To his surprise, she began to cry. He understood: her hatred was the bitter kind spurred by love. Now there was a twist to enliven a story—a crib girl in love with a preacher.

"What do you want me to do about Lybrand?"

"I want you to ruin him, make him so he's no better in folks' eyes than me," she responded, wiping her eyes. "Then people will hate him. Nobody will give money to him anymore or come to his church." She took another drink; some of the liquor ran down her chin and dripped onto her dirty dress.

"You really want to see that happen to him?"

"Yes," she spat, wiping her tears. Her sadness was

becoming anger. "He deserves it. I ain't going to let him do to me what was done before."

"What do you mean?"

"I had a man once. And a baby. They're gone now. My man took my baby and run away. Left me on my own . . . left me nothing but this way to live." She waved her hand, indicating the crib. "I couldn't bear to be left again. I won't let him do that to me."

Byers cleared his throat and decided to open up more to her. Maybe he could shake loose some information more substantial than the mere fact that Lybrand used the services of a prostitute. With what Byers had learned of Lybrand from the packet, and what he further suspected, fornication was probably the man's most minor sin. "Polly—may I call you Polly?—let me tell you a few things. I have received some information in the mail about our good reverend . . . the results of investigation by an old friend of mine back in Chicago. Lybrand is, as you well know, no holy man. Far from it, farther even than you may suspect.

"Back in Chicago, he did just about every common crime you can name—robbery, extortion, swindling, rape. The closest thing to a legitimate profession the man has ever pursued is acting. He received some excellent reviews early in his career. But his best acting has always been done outside the theater. And he's still doing it, pretending to be a clergyman.

"Lybrand is married—several times over, in fact—and he's not had one marriage legally broken except his last one, and that only because his wife died in childbirth. Her maiden name was Viola." He waited to see if that name drew a reaction, but it did not. Obviously Polly Coots didn't keep up with the news, or was too mentally slow to make the connection to the murdered preacher.

So he continued. "At any rate, the child had been conceived before their marriage, and was stillborn well after Lybrand had deserted his wife and gone on to new pursuits. The scandal caused a minor flurry in Illinois, since Lybrand's wife's father was a preacher of some note, named P. D. Viola. Viola was all but destroyed by his daughter's death. He blamed Jason Lybrand for the whole thing.

"And matters only became worse. Reverend Viola's wife died a little while after the daughter did. Grieved herself to death, I suppose. Viola about lost his mind then. He resigned his church and announced to his congregation that he was going to punish the man who had shamed him. He had found out somehow that Lybrand had turned up in Snow Sky, still posing as a preacher. Viola supposedly stood before his congregation and waved a handful of letters, copies of ones he had been mailing to Lybrand, telling him that P. D. Viola was coming like the righteous wrath of God to strike down Lybrand and expose him for what he was. It was a crazy thing to do, because it forewarned Lybrand. But you know how folks can get when they're torn up about something.

"Viola's congregation must have figured he had gone insane . . . which maybe he had. At any rate, it stirred up attention in the Illinois newspapers. NOTED MINISTER OF THE GOSPEL VOWS REVENGE ON YOUNG FAKIR. Quite a story, huh? But listen to this: When P. D. Viola finally showed up in Snow Sky, he was murdered. Beaten to death. Maybe you heard about it. They say they have the man who did it locked up in the jail, but now I've got suspicions that someone else waited by the roadside to kill Viola. Someone who knew he was coming, and who had cause to stop him."

He stopped to let her draw the obvious conclusion herself, but she simply stared at him, almost stupidly. He saw the tragedy in this woman, with her abused body and laudanum-dulled mind. Her future was as gray as the clouds were thick on the horizon outside. For a moment Byers felt an almost forgotten emotion: pity.

"You say he had wives?" she asked.

"Yes."

She silently looked away. Now she seemed sad again rather than angry.

"What was that your note said about cheating his church?" Byers asked.

In a listless voice, she answered, "He's building up a big bunch of money in the bank from the church folks. Going to build a church building, maybe a school, he tells them. But he ain't going to. He's got him two partners who are going to take him into the bank and pretend to make him draw out the money, with him looking scared and all. Then they'll ride off and take him with them like he's their prisoner. They're going to split up the money, and turn him loose. He's going go back and say his life was threatened and the church money stole. The church folk will feel so sorry they'll give even more money to make up for all that was took. Then he'll take it out of the bank again, and this time run off with his partners . . . and me, he told me. Then there would be another town and they'd do it all again. They've done it several other places already, before they came to Snow Sky. They always go to the little towns, the new places where folks won't know them."

"So that's what Lybrand has been doing since he left Chicago!" Byers smiled. Now he was getting some worthwhile information. "Who are his partners?"

She tried to find the names in her dulled mind and could not.

"Ivan Dade and Clure Daugherty, probably," Byers said. "Those names were in the packet—a couple of long-time partners of Lybrand's. Substantially of his ilk but not as sophisticated, according to what the Chicago police told my old newspaper associate." Hesitating, he put out his hand for her to shake.

She did so, limply. Her eyes began to cloud over. "Maybe I shouldn't have said none of this," she said. Suddenly fear came over her. "You won't put in your story that it was me who told on him, will you? If you do, he'll kill me, he will!"

Byers said, "Don't worry—he'll be jailed because of this. He won't be able to hurt you."

"He *will* hurt me! He'll find a way. . . . Oh, why didn't I think of that before? Please don't put my name in your paper!" She began to sob.

"I have no choice," Byers muttered. "Good day." He quickly left the crib. A block away he stopped and looked back. She was standing in the doorway, watching him, wiping tears on her sleeve. For a moment he wanted to go back and reassure her he would do nothing to endanger her, but the moment passed. He went on.

The air smelled wet. Two men walking down the street were talking of the coming storm.

Frogg knelt and whispered to Cochran through the hole in the jail wall. "You'd best be careful about this, Tudor. If the marshal comes back around and catches you here, you'll be sharing this cell with me."

"That marshal's an interesting case," Cochran returned. "He's talking now about how he doesn't think you did it. I really believe he means it."

"I've been getting a similar notion from his way about me—but if he thinks I'm innocent, why don't he let me go?"

Cochran glanced around, feeling exposed there in the alley as he whispered through the gap between the logs. "No evidence in your favor," he said.

"Then why does he think I didn't do it?"

"I don't know. Maybe he thinks I did it. Listen, Hiram—I'm trying to get you some help. Believe it or not, that man Flory sent me after is an old Pinkerton detective. I found him and told him if he'd help clear your name, Flory and me would take that boy off his hands. He's been trying to find a home for him—that's why he's got him."

Frogg whistled softly in surprise. "You're a wilder fool than I took you for, then. What will Flory say?"

"I hope she'll welcome him. But nothing will happen if that detective doesn't agree to my bargain."

"He said no?"

"Not exactly, but he hasn't said yes either. I won't give up, though. He's the best hope we've got."

Frogg said, "The time's fast coming, Tudor, for you to get out of here and leave me to work this out on my own. No point in you getting dragged in. Think of what that would do to Flory. What if that marshal really is starting to suspect you?"

"I'm not leaving you. Don't even suggest it. I wouldn't in any case, and besides, the marshal told me flat out to stay in town."

"Deputy's coming!" Frogg whispered suddenly. Cochran quickly slipped the loose chinking back into place, turned on his heel, and walked rapidly toward the street. At the end of the alley he made a sharp left and ran straight into Polly Coots, knocking her down.

"Sorry, ma'am, I didn't see you there." He reached down and helped her up. Then he saw she had been crying.

"Ma'am, are you all right?"

"I got to go tell him what I did," she said, her voice slurred. "If I tell him then he'll forgive me. I know he will."

Cochran didn't understand the incoherent talk. He smelled gin on her breath. He realized suddenly that this was one of Snow Sky's soiled doves.

Polly walked on, brushing him aside, her head down, butting into the rising wind that swept dust into billows and whirling devils along the street. Cochran watched her go, feeling pity for her.

In the distance a serrated bolt of lightning flashed from cloud to cloud, followed by another that cut a swath to the ground.

A follow-up blast of thunder shook the town, and trailed off. Storm coming in the mountains, Cochran thought. I'd hate to be up there when it hits.

Earl Cobb had managed, when he fell from the bridge, to catch hold of the end of a small evergreen growing almost horizontally out of the side of the gorge. The trunk bent under his weight, swinging him down and against the wet rock wall. His hands slipped on the dampened needles and let him fall. Cobb closed his eyes, expecting to crash into the roiling water below, but he did not. Instead he fell onto a little ledge beneath him. His rifle clattered on down and was lost in the foam that already had swallowed Cap Corley and his horse.

For a few moments there was no noise but that of the waterfall. Cobb lay dazed on the ledge. Groaning, he rolled—the wrong direction. He fell over the edge, barely managing to grab the ledge and stop himself from sliding down the nearly sheer slope into the water.

He looked up. A man appeared above, looking down from the top of the gorge. There was a still-smoking rifle in his hand. A big fellow he was, one Cobb had seen before in town. Clure Daugherty, no doubt.

Daugherty laughed; his voice was remarkably high, almost falsetto. "Got you a good grip there, Marshal?" Then he lifted the rifle and took aim.

Cobb let out a yell and pulled himself up. To his amazement, he made it, and rolled back onto the ledge as the first shot sang down and smacked the rock below him. He rolled into a shallow depression in the wall. It was enough to keep him safely concealed from the rifleman directly above, but left him still dangerously exposed should the man come out onto the bridge.

Cobb reached for his pistol and was relieved to find it still there. His holster thong had a way of slipping off, and he easily could have lost the pistol when he fell. He thumbed off the thong and drew the pistol. The grip was cold and wet in his hand.

"Where is he, Clure?" This was a new voice, coming from somewhere around the near end of the bridge. Daugherty's partner, probably. Cobb scrambled to a squatting position, backed up against the stone wall, and readied himself to shoot should anyone show himself on the bridge.

"He's back up under me," Daugherty said. "I took a shot at him and missed."

"Daugherty!" Cobb yelled. "You're making a bad mistake! You'll get yourself a death sentence if you kill a peace officer!"

"Then it's too late to worry—I already killed your deputy."

Good point for him, bad one for me, Cobb thought.

Dade appeared on the bridge and fired off a quick shot that *spang*ed into the rock directly above Cobb's head. Cobb leveled his pistol and fired quickly in response. Dade ducked back, then returned, firing again. A slug nicked the side of Cobb's leg and another ripped a hole through his sleeve, missing him by a sixteenth of an inch. Cobb fired again, again—and thought he saw Dade spasm once before he withdrew this time.

A silence followed. Smoke from Cobb's pistol floated up from the gorge, mixing with the mist of the churning water. Another gunsmoke cloud dissipated above the bridge where Dade had been.

"I'm hit, Daugherty!" Dade said in a pain-tightened voice. "Plugged me through the arm!"

Daugherty responded in a lower tone; Cobb could

not hear him clearly over the roaring of the water and a new peal of thunder that here in the mountains was twice as loud as it would have been below. He knew, though, that they were making a plan to get to him.

He couldn't stay here, yet he had no way off the ledge. Taking a chance that neither of his assailants would show themselves on the bridge for the next few moments, Cobb emptied the three spent shells from his pistol and replaced them with live ones, then slipped a final one into the cylinder he usually kept empty beneath the hammer. He could not afford an empty cylinder right now.

He groped for a plan. To stay here meant nothing more than draining off his limited ammunition until finally his foes would be able to walk safely out onto the bridge and shoot him at their leisure. But the ledge was a mere lip of rock sticking out at this one place, and even if it had extended farther in either direction, Cobb could not leave the protection of the depression that hid him. He had no desire to take a slug in the crown of his head.

No way out to either side or straight up—leaving only one option: down.

He craned his neck and looked over into the boiling torrent below. The waterfall was close and to his left; its mist was soaking him right now. It crashed onto rocks that were largely obscured by the water. To throw himself down there might mean to impale himself on some upthrusting stone spear or to burst his skull against an unseen, water-covered boulder. He hesitated, unsure.

Two things happened right then. The first was that a tiny avalanche of dirt and gravel fell before Cobb,

letting him know that his two enemies were still directly above. The second was that it began to rain—not a
mild sprinkle, but a gushing storm, as if the water-
gorged belly of some cloud had exploded.

If it was to be done, now was the time. Cobb
stood, took a breath, and lunged forward out of the rock
depression, twisting and firing blindly upward at the
same time. The shot was simply to drive the men above
back away from the edge; there seemed no chance it
would actually strike either one.

Cobb quickly reholstered and restrapped his pistol, took another deep breath, and leapt off the ledge
toward the left, aiming for a small gap between the
edge of the waterfall and the gorge wall, hoping he
could land behind the descending wall of water and be
hidden.

"Yonder he goes, Ivan!" Daugherty yelled. "The
damn fool jumped!"

Dade did not respond and Daugherty looked at
him. Dade had a look of surprise on his face, and his
chest was flooding with bright red blood, washing all
the way to his legs in the rain. Dade wobbled and
turned bedsheet white.

Cobb's unaimed bullet had taken him in the side of
the throat, cutting a path upward to come out below his
right ear. Dade's eyes glazed and he fell limply to his
knees, leaned forward, and silently fell over the edge of
the gorge into the crashing turbulence below.

Chapter 10

Abel Patterson paused, hidden behind a parked wagon, and let Cochran pass on the other side of the street. Cochran strode on to a hotel and entered. Patterson stepped out and began his search again. He noticed the mountains. Raining there—he could see the gray, slanted mist of it in the distance. It would roll into town soon—and it looked like a big storm. Knowing it was coming only increased the sense of pressure he felt to find Spencer.

He reached into his pocket and looked at his watch: almost four o'clock. Spencer had been gone for hours, and still he had not found even a hint of where the boy might have gone. Patterson had dozed off late in a restless night, and when he had awakened in the morning, Spencer's bed was empty. The boy had slipped out and run off.

Patterson knew he probably should have flagged down the innkeeper and recruited him to help with the search, but he didn't really want to talk to Cochran.

Not yet. If he failed to find Spencer on his own, he might have to approach Cochran. At least now he knew where Cochran was staying. He wondered if perhaps Spencer knew too—maybe even was there. If he didn't find Spencer elsewhere, Patterson decided, he would come back and check.

Outside the door of the Pardue Boot Shop Patterson stopped a man with a waxed mustache. "Excuse me— you seen a towheaded boy, about eleven, wandering around, maybe looking lost? New pair of shoes on him."

The man frowned thoughtfully, twitched the mustache as if it moved with the gears of his brain, and finally shook his head. " 'Fraid not. Yours?"

"Sort of."

"Could be he's in O'Brien's Grocery sneaking licorice out of the jar. O'Brien, he lets the younguns get away with that."

It was a possibility. Patterson got directions to the store, thanked the man, and went on.

He was more worried than he would have thought. In one way that made little sense, for Spencer surely had faced much bigger challenges, growing up with an abusive criminal father, than getting by on his own in a mining town. Likely the boy was in his element on the streets—unless his late father had simply kept him penned up in their mountain cabin all his years.

O'Brien's Grocery had four children inside, gathered at the glass-topped candy counter, but none was Spencer. Patterson turned and walked back onto the street, then sat down on the bench on the store porch. He leaned back against the wall and crossed his arms over his broad chest. His longish hair fanned back over his collar.

What really hurts about all this, he thought, is that Spencer ran off only after I suggested that he stay with me for good. I don't know what possessed me to make such a suggestion anyway. I don't have what it takes to raise a boy right. I'm just a worn-out old Pinkerton who can't even locate a lost runt in a mining camp anymore. Can't seem to keep anybody safe in my care—just like I couldn't keep my own brother safe on the streets of Chicago that night.

He stood, listening to the thunder, then walked off the porch and up the center of the street, looking for Spencer in the crowd around him.

He saw the tent church and it gave him a thought. Spencer might have sought out somebody he thought might protect him, like a law officer, or maybe a preacher. The former Pinkerton wasn't inclined to approach the law, given that he didn't know if his absconding with a bag of extortion money had managed to land his name on police dodgers. But the preacher might be worth asking. At the least a clergyman might be willing to keep his eyes and ears open to help out. He might even organize a search if he was a particularly helpful fellow.

Patterson walked to the frame and canvas church and pushed open the door. Gray light from the clouded sky came through the canvas like thin-strained coffee, barely lighting the bench-filled structure, at the front of which stood a crudely made pulpit on a little rostrum, and a small altar table. There was no one and nothing else here.

Patterson stood in the silence a few moments, trying to remember how long it had been since he had set foot in a church, even one as makeshift as this one. A lot of years. Tomorrow was Sunday, he realized.

Lord, he prayed, if you keep Spencer safe and let me find him, maybe I'll come to the service in the morning. Put a few dollars in the plate.

He walked back out onto the street and glanced at the name painted onto the door frame: HOUSE OF PRAYER. Then the name of the minister—JASON LYBRAND.

Lybrand . . . vaguely familiar. Something from the past, from Chicago. Perhaps someone of the same name was in a Pinkerton file. It was not unlikely, given that the Pinkertons never closed a case until the parties involved were either dead, jailed, or cleared.

Patterson buttonholed a passing man. "Where's this preacher Lybrand live?" he asked.

The man singled out the cabin that was Lybrand's. Patterson thanked him and headed for it, glancing again toward the mountains. The wall of rain was moving closer to town. A mist hung in the air. Patterson hurried toward the preacher's cabin.

Lybrand drew back his fist and drove it into Dutch Polly's jaw. The impact made her thin body shudder like a leaf, and knocked her back, where she tottered against a table before sliding to the floor. She cried out and grasped her injured face, tears streaming down her cheeks.

"Oh, Jason, please don't . . . I told you I was sorry!"

"Sorry! Do you know what you've done to me? Flapping your mouth to a newspaperman! You've ruined me! How could you have been such a damned fool?"

"I was mad at you—but I'm sorry now! I came back and said I was sorry, didn't I?"

"You don't know what sorry means yet, my dear! When I'm through with you, you'll have real cause to regret what you've done to me."

She looked at him with honest fear. "Please . . . I wish I hadn't done it. I've thought of nothing but that since I did it!"

Lybrand's lip curled back; he advanced on her. Her tears streamed faster, and she put the back of her hand over her eyes and cowered down on the floor as he bent toward her. His fist went up simultaneously with the knock on his door.

Lybrand froze, lowered his fist, and pointed his thin finger into the prostitute's face. "See? Already he's here! All your crying and sorrow can't fix what's been done. Now you keep quiet—hear me?"

Lybrand straightened his clothing and hair and walked to the door. Rolling his shoulders, twisting his tension-stiffened neck, he opened the door a crack.

Lybrand had seen Oliver Byers in town before and knew the visitor outside was not the newspaperman. This was a tall, broad man with a salt-and-pepper beard.

"Are you the Reverend Lybrand?" Patterson asked.

"I am. What can I do for you?"

"I'd like to speak to you if I could."

"I'm terribly busy at the moment," Lybrand said in an artificially pleasant voice. "I'm in the midst of preparing a difficult sermon, and my home is too strewn about with books and papers to be fit to accept company."

Funny attitude for a preacher, Patterson thought. He said, "I don't want to come in—just to ask you something. My boy is missing. I'm sure he's somewhere in town, but I can't find him. I thought maybe you might have seen him, or be able to help me out some way or another."

Lybrand seemed irritated by the request. Patterson was fast developing the feeling something was amiss here. He had learned in his Chicago years that intuition often ran in advance of reason, like a scout, and flashed warning signals best not ignored.

"I don't know how I can help you," Lybrand said. "Why don't you go to the town marshal?"

"I saw your church tent down there and came up here on impulse." Patterson smiled coolly. "I guess that was a mistake."

"Like I said, I can't help you. I'm sure the boy is fine. Good day. God bless you."

Lybrand abruptly closed the door, leaving Patterson blinking in surprise—and wondering if that in fact had been a flash of skirt and female leg he had seen for half a second in the background as the door swished shut.

Halfway down the hill, he met a man emerging from another cabin. He nodded hello, then asked, "Does the preacher up in that cabin have a wife?"

The man looked up, grinned, and shook his head. "Nope. Surely doesn't." He leaned close. "But the fact is, I've seen one of the town crib harlots sneak up there. What do you think of that out of a preacher, huh?" The man cackled gleefully; obviously he thought the situation was hilarious.

"Not what you expect from a preacher," Patterson said.

"Amen to that! I had him pegged a fake from day one."

Patterson headed back into town through the drizzle to continue his search.

Back in his cabin, Lybrand let his curtain fall back straight. He had been looking covertly around the edge of it, watching Patterson descend. Lybrand had witnessed the brief meeting and conversation of Patterson and the man below, and could tell from their gestures that he was their subject. Maybe talk was out already about him. Maybe that newspaperman had a loose tongue and was mouthing his story even before putting it into print. Lybrand raged inwardly; Polly had ruined him.

She had gotten up and moved to his bed, holding her injured jaw. She sobbed quietly. Dutch Polly had been humiliated often in life, but never so much as now.

She wasn't sure why she had felt so compelled to inform the newspaperman about Lybrand's secret life. Last night and this morning she had been driven by a sense of vengeance. Now that seemed alien; she wanted only Lybrand's affection and forgiveness, and the assurance he would harm her no more.

"That jaw hurt?" he asked her. She thought she detected some tenderness in his voice. Looking up through her tears, she nodded. Without a word, he struck her again.

The pain was more than pain; it spasmed through her in a convulsion like that of a beheaded snake. For a few moments she blacked out. When she came to, she was on the floor, on her back, with Lybrand kneeling beside her.

"You should have never betrayed me," he said. "That's all womenfolk know how to do—to betray. I grew up with a mother who stood by and watched her husband try to destroy her own son, giving no more help than a feeble plea or two. My father might have killed me for all the help she gave. But he couldn't overcome me, Polly. I overcame him in the end . . . just like I'll overcome this Oliver Byers and his little rag newspaper. Nobody has ever been able to destroy me, Polly—not my father, not my mother, not Viola, not Byers, and not you." Then he hit her again.

It all became hellish after that. In the midst of it she stood and tried to run from him on legs wobbly as chicken fat. Repeated blows jolted her, knocking her down again and again, but always she arose. She was keenly aware, for some reason, of the wind moaning around the house. Listening to it, suffering blow after blow, she fell and passed out again.

Daugherty crept along the bank of the gushing stream, cautiously watching the waterfall that was growing bigger and more violent in the rain. Lightning flared and crackled in the sky, and clouds drooped like sodden sponges between the mountains.

The big outlaw still could not believe the marshal had managed to put a bullet through Dade's neck with a randomly fired shot. It was enough to make a man start believing in providence . . . though Daugherty surely didn't want to, especially if providence was on the side of Earl Cobb.

He stopped, standing there in the drenching rain. Maybe the best thing to do was get out of here. Take off across the mountain and let the storm wash away the trail. Most likely the marshal had died when he threw himself toward the waterfall anyway. Daugherty couldn't tell for certain, but it seemed to him that Cobb had made a poor jump and had gone straight into the falls. But maybe he had managed to come up behind—and if so, Daugherty wanted to know it. He didn't want any law close on his tail if he could help it.

Too bad all this had to happen before he, Dade, and Lybrand got around to cleaning out the church bank account down in Snow Sky. Now Dade was gone, Daugherty could not return to town, and the plan was finished. It was Lybrand's fault. Lybrand was just too slow—wait, wait, wait was all he ever would do.

Daugherty mentally voiced his complaint and then put the subject behind him. All that was over now; there was nothing left for him but running. On his own this time.

But not until he knew for sure that the marshal was dead. Daugherty readjusted his hat to make the water sluice off it to the side, and advanced toward the waterfall.

He stopped with a gasp when something rose in the turbulence and vanished. It was Dade, eyes open, white face upturned. No blood on him—all that had washed off. A moment later the corpse reappeared, still facing up, staring at the sky for three or four seconds before washing down again. The body was caught like a leaf in a circular up-and-down movement of water created by the nearby falls and the shape of the rocks below. Daugherty shuddered.

He advanced again. The waterfall roared like an angry devil.

No movement that looked human, no voice, nothing. For all Daugherty could tell, he was alone here. By himself with nothing but dead men around. He wondered if the marshal might have washed down the stream like the deputy who had plunged off the bridge.

The outlaw backed up against the side of the gorge as he neared the waterfall. Only a narrow gap between the wall of water and the rock around it was there to allow access to the area behind the falls. If Cobb was hidden anywhere, it had to be there.

Daugherty stopped suddenly, and grinned. If Cobb was back there, waiting to surprise him, then Daugherty had his own surprise to hand out first. He swung the rifle around at hip level and swept the falls with bullets. With any luck, if Cobb was back there he took one or two of them, mortally.

Daugherty hugged the wall and reloaded, then advanced with more confidence. At the least Cobb would now be spooked. The outlaw reached the edge of the falls, held his breath, and rushed on through the gap.

Now he was behind the plunging water, on a sandy, gravelly patch shielded by an arch of rock. The falls were to Daugherty's right, a curtain of water blocking all view of the world on the other side.

No Earl Cobb. The moist little enclave, dark as late twilight, was empty. Daugherty breathed in relief. Obviously Cobb had been washed under the falls when he jumped. That meant he was dead.

The outlaw nodded in satisfaction and lowered his rifle. At that moment his eye fell on the wet sand and gravel beneath him.

Tracks. Fresh. Cobb's tracks.

Movement beside him—and Cobb came out of a shadowed crevice in the rock. Cobb's pistol swung around in an arc and laid open Daugherty's jaw. Blood and a scream came out of the big man's mouth. He lifted his rifle. Cobb grasped its barrel and pushed it aside before Daugherty could fire. When the outlaw did get off a shot it ricocheted off the stone behind them and out through the waterfall. As it did, Cobb shoved backward on the rifle. Daugherty danced clumsily and then stumbled into the falls. The water grabbed him like a clutching hand and pulled him in.

Cobb let go of the rifle so Daugherty would fall in without taking him with him, but Cobb's sleeve was torn and Daugherty's rifle caught in the tear. Cobb, already unsettled because of the fight, found himself dragged into the water with Daugherty.

They came up together on the other side. Both had lost their weapons. Daugherty's face was bleeding, turning the foam around him pink. The outlaw saw the marshal bob to the surface and let out a lionlike roar. Daugherty's stone of a fist shot up from the water and caught Cobb on the side of the head.

Cobb absorbed the blow well, but it did daze him. He pulled away, trying to get a grip on a rock to avoid being swept away. But what he took for a good handhold actually was a badly fractured and eroded stone, and as he grabbed it a big fragment snapped off in his hand. Cobb was pulled downstream, then sucked under.

Beneath the water he found himself struggling with Daugherty—struggling, but Daugherty wasn't struggling back. He opened his eyes, and in the foaming water saw that it was not Daugherty at all, but Daugherty's partner. The man was dead, a bullethole in his neck. He couldn't believe it—that wild shot he had fired off when he jumped must have actually hit this fellow. There was one for the books.

Suddenly Cobb's head broke water and he sucked in a lungful of air. The corpse came up, headed back down, and Cobb was pulled after it. He groped out blindly and managed to get a grip on a firm rock this time. Pulling upward, straining his arm terribly, he drew himself out of the circling current that was moving the corpse in an endless cycle.

Cobb wrapped his arms around the stone that held him and drew in more air. The storm was going full fury, pelting the water all around him. Lightning flashed and Cobb saw Daugherty's face appear before him, rising from the water.

Dead? Maybe so. Daugherty was pale as a bedsheet, and his eyes were closed. But a moment later a big arm rose from the water and grabbed the same rock to which Cobb held. Daugherty's eyes opened; his lips drew back to expose his teeth like those of a snarling animal. The gash Cobb had inflicted on his face looked hideous.

Daugherty swore at Cobb and with his free arm went for the marshal's throat. Cobb lunged out almost blindly and connected with Daugherty's forehead. New blood gushed down Daugherty's face as Cobb heard the crunch of rock against bone. He had forgotten that the broken-off shard of rock from his first failed handhold was still gripped in his hand. It had done the job well. Cobb knew even as Daugherty let go of the rock and slipped beneath the water that the man was dead.

Suddenly Cobb's head began to spin. Pain rippled a dull electric path through his frame. It felt like he might have bruised some ribs somewhere along the way. He dropped the piece of rock that had killed Daugherty and held to his perch with both arms, but he was growing weaker. In the lightning glare he watched

Daugherty's body wash down the stream, and then his own eyes closed and he slid beneath the water.

When Dutch Polly awoke it was dark in the room except for a circle of light cast by a lamp on Lybrand's table. He was seated there, drinking, looking at her hatefully.

"Back around for some more, huh?" he said. His voice was slightly slurred, either by liquor or the distortion of her own ringing ears.

"No . . ." she said as he rose and walked to her. She tried to stand but fell back onto the floor. He hit her and she began crying again.

He cursed her and kicked her. This time she managed to get up. She stumbled toward the door but, staggering to one side, reached the window instead. Grabbing out for something to balance her, she pulled down the curtain and rod. It was dark outside. She had been unconscious a long time. The rain pounding the windows was fierce. A lightning flash lit the terrain outside, and in its glare the heavens gave Dutch Polly the last gift she would ever receive: a final glimpse of the world she was about to depart.

Cursing at her now for having pulled down the curtain, Lybrand grasped her shoulders and pulled her back, then pushed hard. She screeched and spun against the table; the impact made a horrible smashing sound.

Lybrand fumbled with the curtain, feeling exposed, and finally got it back in place. Still swearing, he turned to renew his abuse of Polly.

Something in the way she lay stopped him in his

tracks. He looked closely at her—no breath. No movement. Panic rising, he dropped to his knees and crawled to her. Rolling her over, he saw her eyes stare up at his, but there was no light, no life in them. He had killed her.

He pulled back up from her and clasped his hands together, then drew his shoulders up tight around his neck, taking the tense posture of a child at bedside prayers. Polly's head rolled to the side and she seemed to look at him again, blood dripping from the corner of her slightly open mouth. Lybrand stared at her, trying to figure out if he had killed her intentionally or by accident. He wasn't sure it really mattered. Dead was dead.

He returned to the window and peeped through the curtain. Lightning showed him an empty town below. The handful of cabins near his were shut tight; lights burned in only a couple. Thank heaven for the storm. Many people, apparently, had turned in early because of it. The street flares were out, and even the saloons, dance halls, and restaurants had apparently closed, their proprietors probably huddling now in the safer confines of their squatty log cabins.

No need to worry, he told himself. No one is out there tonight. No one saw what happened. I'm safe. In fact, maybe I can use this storm to my advantage.

Got to get rid of her body, make it look like she died somewhere else, some other way. . . .

His mind clicking off a new plan, Lybrand let the curtain fall, and thus did not see Spencer Vestal dart from beneath the overhanging evergreen branches of a tree not thirty feet from the cabin. The tree had kept the runaway boy somewhat dry, but no longer was he willing to stay there, for he knew something bad had happened in that cabin. He himself had lived with abuse long enough to know the sound of it when he heard it—and that familiar sound, though muffled, had been audible from inside. He had seen the woman at the window, the man dragging her back. After that there had been no sound at all, and that made Spencer even more afraid, for he feared the woman was dead. He could feel death in his marrow, smell it in the wet air.

He ran back down toward the town in the rain.

Chapter 11

Earl Cobb had come back to the living about sunset.

Rain on his face was the first thing he was aware of. The second was that he hurt quite a lot. He was crumpled awkwardly on the bank of the stream, where he had washed up—with his nose turned toward the sky rather than buried in the water, to his good fortune. It took him a long time to gather the courage to move, and when he did he was both sorry and gratified: the former because the movement brought him pain, the latter because he could move at all.

Cobb got up carefully, slowly, and examined himself. At the same time he pulled together his memories of what had happened here. He remembered the death of Cap Corley and felt a stab of sorrow that hurt as much as his battered frame. At least Cap had not left behind a family to grieve for him.

When Cobb tried to walk he found it brought wracking pain. His left ankle throbbed. After only a few steps he sank to the earth again, coming down in a gathering pool of rain. Falling down made his damaged ribs hurt that much worse. Lightning sizzled through the atmosphere and tinged the air with a clean electric smell.

New wet-weather waterfalls gushed here and there around him as the mountain shed the falling rain. Silver Falls was massive now, hammering water against rock with terrible force. Down in town, Cobb figured, Bledsoe Creek surely was gushing to its limits. Possibly some of the streets would flood.

Cobb was still down in the gorge, the storm was still raging, and the stream was rising. Good thing he had come to when he had. Even now he had best get out or his feet might be knocked from under him, and in the shape he was, it was even money whether he would be able to get out of the water if he fell into it.

He remembered the Apex McCall cabin, where Daugherty and Dade apparently had been holing up. There he could wait out the storm, and in the morning make it back down to Snow Sky—if he wasn't too sore to move by then.

The cabin was, at the moment, to Cobb's right, on the far side of the gorge from Snow Sky. The slope on that side was far too steep for him to climb. The other side was much less so, though it was across the stream. Now this was a fine fix: either climb a nearly sheer rock wall in the rain, with a busted ankle and banged-up ribs, or try to wade a gushing stream that obviously was trying to fill its year's quota for dead men.

"Ain't been your day, Cobb," he said to himself. With that he put out a foot and stepped, with much pain and wincing, onto one of the rocks thrusting out of the rising stream, his idea being to cross to the more shallow bank, climb it, and double back to the bridge, where he could cross to the side where the cabin stood.

"So far so good," he said. He stepped again, reaching another rock, and from there half stepped, half fell onto another, this one a long slab buried sideways in the water. On it he made it three quarters of the way to the other side, pain shooting up his leg with every careful step.

But from there on there were no rocks on which to step. Cobb stood, feeling both ludicrous and frightened there on the rock in the stream, rising water lapping at his toes as the storm sizzled through the mountains around him.

"Here goes," he said.

Sitting on the rock, he slid on his rump into the water, praying it was not as deep as it looked.

It was. Cobb was pulled under at once and washed fifteen feet downstream before he could find the surface again. When he pulled his face out of the water he was clinging to a big log, part of a tangle of other logs wedged among the rocks.

"What the—" Suddenly he realized it: This was the bridge, or the remnants of it. Sometime while he was unconscious, the rickety structure had yielded to the pounding water and washed away. He twisted his head and looked at the far side of the gorge. Too high. No way to reach the top and the cabin.

"Well, Cobb, looks like you're going to make a nighttime trip to Snow Sky after all," he said to himself.

Painfully he worked his way along the timber rubble to the bank, where he pulled himself out. After another ten minutes of slow, agonizing climbing, he made it up the shallow bank and back onto the trail that led down the mountain to Snow Sky.

"I'd best find myself some sort of crutch," he said aloud.

He had to limp a long way before he finally found a crotched sapling that might make a decent crutch. Propping up in the driving rain, he dug his folding knife from his pocket. Night was falling now, and he had to strain to see what he was doing. It took a long time to cut, twist, and break away a makeshift crutch, and when finally he had, he found the crutch wobbly and prone to slide on the wet rocks. Still, it was better than having no extra support at all.

The storm was terrific, and lightning danced around him. Cobb had never been much afraid of lightning, but from the way bolts were firing out of the sky, he could almost suspect the heavenly host was holding a turkey shoot, with him as the prize bird.

Oh Lord above, Cobb prayed inwardly, I surely hope I make it. Please let me make it.

He began walking. Water bounded past his feet toward the base of the mountain. His improvised crutch slid and almost failed him. Cobb prayed for the storm to slacken, but it did not. Town seemed a long way off.

Cochran cautiously answered his door. The caller was Abel Patterson, standing there drenched from rain, staring back at Cochran without expression.

"Hello," Cochran said. "This is a surprise."

"Is he here?" Patterson asked, walking in without waiting for an invitation. He swept off his hat, in the process flinging about a pint of water off it onto the floor. Another quart drained off his slicker, leaving a watery trail across the room. It hardly mattered; the roof was leaking at three places anyway.

"Well, is he here?" Patterson asked again.

"I don't know what you mean."

"Don't you? Are you saying Spencer hasn't been here?"

"No, he hasn't. Is he gone?"

"Since this morning. I've looked for him all day. Not a sign. I thought maybe he had found you. You're the only other man in Snow Sky he knows at all."

"Well, I wouldn't say he knows me, just from staying at my inn. In any case, he didn't come here. Did you tell him the bargain I offered you?"

Patterson wouldn't meet Cochran's eye. "No. Instead I asked him if he would let me keep him, raise him. I never thought I'd reach the point of wanting anything like that, but that boy has a way of growing on you."

Patterson now looked at Cochran. "He's got scars on him, you know. He's lucky he survived his childhood. He had no mother when I ran across him, and he had just lost his father, poor excuse for one though he was." Patterson stopped, then fought out the rest of what he had decided to say. "That boy needs a good raising. I'm accepting your offer."

Cochran drew a deep breath. "He'll get a good raising, Mr. Patterson. That I pledge to you. But first we'll have to find him. Do you have any idea where he might go?"

"I don't. I suppose he's just hiding out somewhere.

I'm worried. A stormy night's no time for a boy to be roaming loose in a mining camp."

Cochran said, "I'll get my hat and coat. We'll find him together."

———————————◆———◆———◆———————————

Bledsoe Creek was more like a river now, raging through Snow Sky like a mad beast. Brush, leaves, trash, scraps of lumber, and occasional drowned animals came sweeping along its angry current.

Less than a yard above the rising surface of the rushing water, Spencer Vestal perched. He was inside an outhouse—one of several built at the end of the platforms that extended out from the creek bank and over the water. It wasn't the most sanitary way to dispose of human wastes, but it was efficient, legal, common to mining camps, and preferable to another system many people used: dumping their raw sewage out the back door.

Spencer was glad to at least be dry. He had never been afraid of storms; he even liked them, partly because his despised father had not. But this storm was the worst Spencer had seen. Several sheds now were flat, several porch roofs completely blown off, and a few house roofs on the verge of going the same way—but this outhouse above the creek was shrugging off the weather rather well. It shook a bit in the wind and had one small leak in its roof, but Spencer felt safe here.

Before finding this little refuge, he had considered returning to Abel Patterson. Now he was glad he had not; he did not want to go back to Patterson for fear he would never be free of him again if he did. He knew

Patterson cared for him more deeply all the time, and wanted the best for him, but he also knew what he really needed: a mother. He did not want to spend another day being raised by a man alone. He had experienced enough of that.

He could barely remember his own mother, but he clearly recalled that her touch was soft and loving, and that she did not beat and curse him as his father did. A new father Spencer could take—if he was kind and caring—or leave, as long as a loving mother came with the bargain. And that woman at the Cochran Inn, the one he had heard worried for him, would do just fine. When the storm was over, Spencer decided, he would try to find the man who apparently was her husband, and if he could not find him, he would walk all the way back to that inn on his own, and ask that woman to become his mother. If he had the courage.

Spencer tried to think about how nice it would be to have a mother again, but that pleasant thought kept giving way to memory of the horrible encounter he had witnessed a little earlier through that cabin window. He wondered if the poor woman being so beaten was someone's mother—and if she somehow might have survived. He felt reasonably sure she had not.

He looked down through the hole of the outhouse and watched the rising water below. If it kept getting higher he would have to leave here; the outhouse might be swept away. Turning, he stepped to the door and cracked it. Looking out, he saw that the rain was continuing, a little slackened from before, but not much.

Something moved out in the rain. Pulling the door almost completely closed, Spencer squinted. A lightning flash revealed what it was: a man, walking through the storm, carrying something on his shoulder. The thing apparently was heavy and wrapped in a blanket. The next lightning flash brought Spencer a shudder, for he realized that the man was the one he had seen pulling the woman away from the cabin window, and the thing on his shoulder was a body. Her body.

Eyes wide, Spencer watched the man descend to the creek. Spencer now noticed a coil of rope over the man's other shoulder. When the man passed out of Spencer's view, the boy closed the outhouse door and went to a knothole on the side wall. Pressing his face to the hole, blinking against the rain that battered in against his eye, he watched the man proceed on to a similarly constructed outhouse a few yards up the creek.

The man looked around furtively, then went inside the outhouse with his burden. When he came out again about a minute later, he had only the blanket and rope in hand. He tossed the blanket into the creek, where it twisted and swirled away downstream on the current.

The man then stepped down into the edge of the roiling stream himself, gripping the outjutting beams that supported the outhouse. He worked his way slightly beneath the structure, the water swirling to his waist and threatening to pull him out into the stream. As Spencer watched, the man looped the rope firmly around one of the two tree-trunk poles that provided the main support of the outhouse.

The man struggled back up onto the bank again. Holding both ends of the rope firmly, he began to pull in the same direction the pole already was being pushed by the current. Spencer heard the creak of the moving timber. He realized how fortunate he was that he had hidden in this privy and not that one; he could not guess what the man would have done had he found a little boy looking back at him when he opened the door.

Lightning danced through the sky, turning darkness to day and then returning it to darkness. Bit by bit the pole support leaned, and then with a wrench pulled free. The man fell back onto his rump, still holding the rope. The horizontal outhouse supports sagged downward, pulling up on one side from the muddy, weakened bank. The outhouse descended partially into the water. The man rose and went to the other side, where he apparently loosened the remaining support pole, for although Spencer could not see him there, suddenly the tilting outhouse fell completely into the creek, broke loose from its platform, and was caught in the rush of the stream. It began to sink even before it swept out of Spencer's view.

Spencer crept around to the other side of the outhouse, but could find no opening through which to watch the damaged little building wash down the creek. He returned to the knothole on the other side and looked back out.

The man was gone. He had taken his rope with him.

———————◆━◆━◆———————

Cobb made it almost to Snow Sky before he collapsed. He had reached the place almost at the base of the mountain where the way leveled off across a narrow plateau, and from there descended toward two hills and the footbridge across Bledsoe Creek.

The marshal lay still for a minute, then got up

again. The rain had nearly stopped, but the creek was higher than ever as water hammered down from the mountain. He continued, slowly, until at last he passed between the twin hills and saw Snow Sky.

The town, illuminated by the now more sporadic bursts of lightning, looked much abused by the weather. Canvas flapped, brush and limbs lay strewn everywhere, and fallen trees lay across woodsheds and telegraph wires. Cobb saw all that in the momentary flashes of light. To him the battered town was beautiful, for the mere fact he was seeing it reminded him he had cheated death.

But he was terribly weak and his ankle hurt worse than ever. Cobb feared he might collapse in exhaustion.

He began his walk toward the creek. The trail was slick and wet, and his crutch slipped. With a yell he fell onto his back.

He dragged himself the rest of the way to the footbridge. He blacked out a few moments, then awakened suddenly and realized his face had been all but submerged in a puddle. He considered how ironic it would have been to survive a gun battle and a long, lightning-lit descent down a mountainside in the worst storm he had seen in a decade—only to then drown in two inches of puddle water.

His crutch lay beside him, and he used it to push himself up. Grasping the handrail of the bridge, he began working his way across, his vision unfocused and dim.

That was why he did not see that one section of the footbridge was no longer there. The gorged creek had swept a loose section away. Cobb put his crutch out for one more step, and it pierced the surface of the still-rising creek. He fell straight forward into the water.

The experience was something like being buried in a grave, but not a normal, hole-in-the-earth one. This grave was out of a nightmare. Instead of dank earth around you, there was liquid darkness that turned you like a roasting duck on a spit. Cobb groped out beneath the water, finding nothing, feeling himself carried along in a silent rush. He had no idea which way was up, which was down.

Got to relax, he thought. Got to let myself rise.

But relaxing wasn't easy, for he hadn't been prepared for his tumble into the water and thus hadn't drawn in a deep breath. He longed for air. Got to relax. Got to relax if ever I want another breath.

Suddenly he broke the surface. He threw back his head and took in a big gulp of air before being pulled back down again. Only a moment later he slammed into something hard. For a few seconds he was pinned to a flat surface by the current, like a butterfly smashed flat against a window in a windstorm. His hands found a corner; he got a grip and pulled up.

He was on the edge of a smashed little shed of some sort, jammed firmly up against rocks on the edge of the stream. He managed to drag himself, by some amazing gift of strength, atop the little building, which appeared to be lying on its back in the water. There had been a door on the front of it, but it had been ripped away by the current. Cobb, panting, laid himself on the now-horizontal front beside the dark, rectangular opening where the door had been. He could tell from the solid feel of the wood surface beneath him that the building was firmly lodged and would go nowhere.

Lord, I'm tired, Cobb thought. If it's all right with you and my guardian angel, I'll rest here for a moment. Not for long, I promise . . . just for a moment. . . .

His eyes closed and he passed out, lying flat atop the tight-wedged little building, his body in the space between the door and the edge of the wall. His left hand slipped over and dangled into the water inside the outhouse, where Dutch Polly's hair floated out from her upstaring corpse to brush his unfeeling fingers in the current.

Oliver Byers rolled over in his bed and resettled himself. He dreamed of being at the office, working with his noisy old hand press. It thumped and knocked, irritating him as always. When it made a particularly loud bump, Byers opened his eyes, and knew that the noise was not a product of his dream, and that he was not alone in his house. He sat up, looking into the darkness.

A match flared, moved, touched the wick of a lamp. Byers drew in his breath as the light revealed Jason Lybrand, soaked in rain, his hair matted on his forehead.

"You're Oliver Byers, I believe," Lybrand said. "Oliver Byers the newspaperman."

Byers wished he had kept his own pistol within reach of his bed. Instead it was in a drawer all the way across the room.

"What are you doing in my house? Get out of here!" Byers stormed.

Lybrand laughed in an ugly way. "Get out? Why? I

hear you might want to talk to me, newspaperman. I hear you've already done some talking about me, behind my back. Well, here I am. You want your interview? Take your chance! Or maybe you don't want to talk to me. Maybe you planned to print up stories about me without even asking me about them."

Byers said, "You get out of my house."

Lybrand did not move.

Byers, becoming more frightened by the second, decided that the truth he normally valued so highly perhaps wasn't the best option at the moment. "I haven't been speaking to anybody about you. Why should I? I don't know what you're talking about." He hoped to the heavens Lybrand would believe this.

But the intruder simply shook his head. "You needn't lie. Dutch Polly Coots came to me and told me what she had done," Lybrand said. "She told me you said you already had something on me you were ready to put into your newspaper." Lybrand paused. His eyes flashed. "She said you told her you think I killed P. D. Viola."

Byers knew he could not lie his way out now. "Look," he said, "I'm sorry. Just forget all this and I'll do the same."

"She said you told her you had something on me that had come in the mail." Lybrand reached behind him. When he brought his hand around again it held a knife that flashed in the lamplight. "Where is it?"

Dutch Polly obviously had picked up more of what he had told her that Byers would have thought. "There's nothing, I swear!" he said.

"Where?" Lybrand smiled and leaned forward, turning the blade for Byers to see. "You might as well tell me, Byers, because I'll find that information even if you don't, even if I have to burn down this house and your newspaper office." He paused. His face became ugly with contempt. "Ah, hell with it, hell with you. You're right about me. When this week started I had never killed another man. Then I had to kill Viola. A little while ago I rid the world of Dutch Polly. . . . That's right, I killed her, too. Two killings in one week. A third won't clutter up things much worse."

Byers moaned, drew back. "The packet—it's in my file, in the office."

"Thank you. You've saved me some time." Lybrand lifted the knife.

"Please . . . please . . ."

"Don't beg. It doesn't become a grown man to beg."

Byers scrambled backward and slid off the bed. He dived for the drawer that held his pistol.

Lybrand was on him before he could even reach it. The knife stabbed down; Byers cried out and fell. He rolled onto his back, clutching his shoulder, looking fearfully into Lybrand's unsmiling face.

"Too bad you won't be around to write up your own obituary," Lybrand said.

The knife descended and Byers screamed.

Chapter 12

Lybrand's head was reeling and he felt he might faint. Hidden in darkness, he clung to a tree behind the *Argus* office and tried to calm himself. He had found Byers' slaying distressing, much more so than the murder of Viola. Maybe it was because he was still edgy from killing Dutch Polly, though that had been as much accident as outright murder.

Byers had died too noisy a death; that was the problem. His screams had been upsetting, but also dangerous. Lybrand hoped the newspaperman's cries had not roused any neighbors. Fear of that had forced Lybrand to flee after only three stabs; he would have liked to have stayed longer to be fully sure Byers was dead.

Only a soft drizzle remained from the storm, and even that was diminishing. No more lightning flashed, and the thunder was just a distant grumbling, gone on to other parts.

After a few minutes Lybrand began to feel better. The fainting feeling passed, to be replaced by weariness. But there could be no rest yet. He went to the back door of the newspaper office; as he expected, it was locked. Looking around to make sure no one was about, he picked up a stone, wrapped it in a handkerchief, and as quietly as possible broke out a pane of the door's window. He reached in and opened the latch, then let out a faint yelp and pulled back his hand. He had cut it on the broken glass. Swearing softly, he wrapped the handkerchief around the cut to stanch the blood. He opened the door and entered the office.

Patterson shook his head. "It's no good, Cochran. It's taking too long, and Spencer could be anywhere."

"Then let's divide and look separately," Cochran suggested. "Either of us finds him, we take him back to my room and wait for the other."

The rain-soaked pair split up, Cochran heading back toward Bledsoe Creek, Patterson continuing to explore the main part of town.

After several more minutes of fruitless searching, Patterson turned down Silver Street and passed the Silver Striker Saloon and the San Juan Sign Company, and there stopped. He was at the office of the Snow Sky *Argus*, and he had seen movement inside it. He noticed through the front window that the door apparently was slightly open.

He circled the building and approached the back door carefully. It creaked open at his touch. "Spencer?" he asked as he stepped inside.

Patterson dug out a match and struck it. Simultaneously with the flare he saw a man near him, the face covered partially by a hand. A hard fist struck Patterson on his bearded jaw and he fell, stunned. His attacker ran; Patterson saw that he had a packet beneath his arm.

"Hey!" Patterson shouted. "Come back here!" He dived after the fleeing man and caught his ankle. The man fell, hitting hard, driving the breath from him.

Patterson jumped atop him, pinning him. The man struggled, still clinging to his packet. He had a handkerchief wrapped around one hand.

"Figure a storm's a good cover to rob somebody— that it?" Patterson said. He didn't bother to wonder why he even cared; years of Pinkerton work had ingrained a get-involved attitude into him when it came to crime.

Suddenly the pinned man rolled and swung up a fist, hitting Patterson in the jaw. The ex-Pinkerton was knocked back, and the man beneath him writhed and pulled free. Patterson grabbed for him again and missed, but he did manage to grab the packet. It tore, and something fell out. The man put his hand over the tear and ran as hard as he could out of the office and down the street.

Patterson stood slowly, rubbing his jaw and working his mouth from side to side. He thought about chasing the man down, but decided he had best concentrate on finding Spencer.

He had caught only a glimpse of the man's face, but it seemed familiar. Where had he seen him before? He rubbed his jaw again and glanced down.

At his feet lay a bloodied handkerchief. Must have come off his hand, Patterson thought. That fellow had a wound.

He stepped over and picked up what had fallen

from the torn packet. It was a photograph—the same man he had just fought, dressed in some sort of frontier costume, a fur hat on his head. He was on a stage. Now Patterson recognized him: the preacher Jason Lybrand, the one who had acted so cold toward him when he came asking about Spencer.

Now, there was a mystery. What would a preacher be doing breaking into a newspaper office in the night? Patterson put the photograph in his pocket. He stepped out the back door and started around toward the street, and as he did so he happened to look up the hill toward the nearest cabin. Something moved in its doorway. Patterson squinted but could not make out what it was.

"Spence?" He headed toward the cabin at a lope, then heeled to a stop when he saw the moving thing was not Spencer, but another man, dragging himself out of the door.

Patterson approached him. "You drunk or hurt?"

The man groaned and lifted a hand. Patterson pulled his box of matches from his pockets and struck another light. The wind snuffed the match after only a moment, but in that moment Patterson saw enough.

The man's hand was drenched in blood. Patterson couldn't help but marvel at what a mind-boggling night this was turning out to be.

He knelt at the man's side. "You shot?"

"Cut . . . stabbed . . ."

"Who?"

"Lybrand . . . Jason Lybrand."

Patterson glanced down at the newspaper office. "That your office down there?"

"Yes . . ."

"I'm getting you back inside."

"No . . . got to get the packet . . . before Lybrand does. . . ." Byers could barely speak.

"He's already got a packet, so the odds are you're too late. I'm taking you inside, like it or not. You'll die otherwise."

Carefully he lifted Byers, who promptly passed out, and carried him inside. He lay him on the bed. A lamp already burned in the room.

Byers opened his eyes. "Abel Patterson—it's you!"

Patterson frowned. "How do you—"

"Listen to me, Patterson. It was Lybrand who killed the preacher Viola . . . said he killed Polly Coots, too."

"Killed Viola—"

"Yes . . ."

"Who's Polly Coots?"

"Town prostitute—in love with Lybrand. . . . He said he killed her. Now he's killed me, too."

"Not yet he hasn't. You're still with us, friend. I'm going to get you some help."

"Too late. You go after him, Patterson . . . get Lybrand for me . . ."

"But how do you know who I am?"

Byers did not answer. He closed his eyes and let out a slow breath. He did not take another.

Patterson pulled a blanket across Byers' face.

Cochran, standing near Bledsoe Creek, could just make out the overturned outhouse in the water, and a man atop it. Moving now, he was. The front of the outhouse was barely above the surface of the creek, making the man appear to be lying on the water itself. Cochran heard him groan, saw him stir again.

"Are you all right?" Cochran called, drawing near to the bank. The outhouse was lodged on the far side of the creek from him.

The man groaned once more and slid off into the water.

Without hesitation, Cochran splashed out after him. He miscalculated the creek's depth and went under as soon as he reached its middle. Floundering, he found the base of the outhouse underwater. Something touched his face. He reached for it. A foot.

He grabbed it, thinking at first it was that of the man who had fallen in the water, but then he realized this foot was far too small. And it was bare and cold— cold as the foot of a corpse. With that thought Cochran let go of it quickly. He pushed up on the base of the submerged shack and came to the surface. Pulling up on top of the shack, he caught his breath and looked for the man who had fallen.

He saw the man dragging himself up on the bank, and was surprised to see it was Earl Cobb. Remembering his underwater discovery, Cochran looked down into the vacant, upturned door of the outhouse and saw a murky shape inside, below the surface of the water. Summoning his courage, he reached down. His hand closed on sodden cloth; he pulled up.

A woman's pale face, eyes open, emerged for a moment from the water. Cochran shouted and let her go, then fell backward into the creek. He splashed quickly to the bank and pulled up beside the marshal.

"There's a dead woman in there!" he exclaimed.

Cobb groaned, then said, "Mr. Cochran, I've had

quite a long and difficult day." He obviously had not grasped what Cochran had said.

"But Marshal, there's a—"

Cochran stopped, for on the other side of the creek he saw the shadowy little figure of Spencer Vestal, looking at him. Cochran whipped off his spectacles, shook the water from them, and put them on again. It really was Spencer.

"Mister?" the boy said. His voice was so soft Cochran could barely hear it. Cochran stood. "Wait there, Spencer. I've been looking for you."

Cochran splashed out into the water, its temperature and his awareness of the corpse making him shudder.

Halfway across he saw Abel Patterson running toward Spencer from behind, waving his hand. Obviously Patterson had just now spotted him. Spencer whirled, saw Patterson, and ran away into the darkness.

"Wait!" Patterson shouted. "Come back, Spencer!"

By now Cochran had reached the bank and Spencer was fully out of view. Cochran and Patterson ran after him, looking all about, but the night was too dense; they could not see him.

"Hiding from us!" Patterson said. "I don't understand it."

"Neither do I," Cochran said. "He actually called to me a moment ago, like he wanted me to come."

Patterson said nothing for a while. He looked at Cochran. "It's obvious, then. It isn't both of us he's running from. Just me."

Cochran said, "Do you know there's blood all over your shirt, Mr. Patterson?"

Cobb, despite his injuries, was in surprisingly good condition. Cochran and Patterson together helped him down the street toward the jail. Patterson was edgy around the lawman, but felt obliged to help.

"Cap Corley is dead," Cobb said. "Shot down. Them who did it are dead, too."

"It's been quite a night for dying," Patterson muttered so low the others did not notice.

"How'd you wind up on top of that outhouse, Marshal?" Cochran asked.

"That I can't rightly remember."

"There's a dead woman inside it," Cochran said.

"Good Lord!" Cobb said. Patterson could have provided another grisly surprise, but decided to wait. Oliver Byers was beyond human help, in any case.

They reached the jail; Patterson pounded the door. In a moment it opened, and Heck Carpenter looked out. The deputy obviously had not slept at all, nor changed clothing for many hours. When he saw Cobb, his eyes went big and bright.

"Marshal! Thank heaven! I thought you were surely dead and gone!"

"I ain't dead. But Cap is."

"Dead! What happened?"

"Get me to bed and maybe in a bit I can tell you," Cobb said. "In the meantime, Heck, there's a privy in the creek that needs cleaning out." Then Cobb almost collapsed; Patterson caught him.

Heck looked at the others. "Privy? Is he delirious or something?"

They helped Cobb to his bed, and Heck freed a sobered-up drunk and sent him after Walt Chambers. Patterson and Cochran stepped outside. The eastern mountains were backlit by the coming dawn. "Sun will be up in a couple of minutes. I'll go looking for Spencer again," Cochran said.

"I'm coming too," Patterson said.

"No. I think I should go alone. Remember how he ran when he saw you? I know it's hard to take, but it's obvious he's just going to keep running as long as you're after him."

Patterson knew Cochran was right.

"All right. You go alone. I know when I don't belong." At that moment he would have been willing to give away every cent of that fifty thousand in the back across town just to feel like Spencer wanted him instead of someone else.

Patterson stepped off the porch. "By the way, Cochran—there's still another dead body to be dealt with. Don't know his name, but he runs the paper here. He was murdered. He's lying on a bed in a house behind the paper office. I found him and put him there."

Patterson walked away, leaving Cochran wondering if it was some gruesome joke. Finally he shrugged. "I guess that explains the bloody shirt," Cochran wryly said to himself. He turned and went back into the jail office to report what Patterson had just told him. Behind him the sun spilled fresh light onto the weather-battered town.

Patterson walked back toward the creek, bitter at Spencer's latest rejection. Never should have let that boy come to mean anything to me, he thought. Care about somebody, and you're bound to hurt when you lose them. Just like when Roland died.

Patterson drew close to Bledsoe Creek. Several men were fishing Dutch Polly's body out of the water.

The people gathered around were silent as pallbearers. The prostitute's body was a ghastly sight when it came out of the water, even from the distance Patterson saw her from. Someone had quickly covered her with a sheet.

Patterson started to walk on, but something made him stop. After a pause, he went to the crowd, pushed through, and knelt beside the body. He pulled back the sheet and looked at Polly's face.

"Hey—there's no call for that," someone said.

Patterson did not seem to hear. He put the sheet back in place and rose. "She was a whore?" he asked.

Someone protested the frank question, but another answered. Yes, she was a whore, name of Dutch Polly Coots. Must have gone into the outhouse to get away from the storm, and it washed away and drowned her.

"She didn't drown," Patterson said. He had seen enough bodies in his time to know. "She was hit in the head."

"No loss either way," one of the cruder members of the crowd said. "She was just a whore."

Patterson did not respond. He turned and walked away. The crowd parted to let him through.

Lybrand also had watched from a distance as Dutch Polly's body was fished out of the waterlogged outhouse.

He was in turmoil. Should he stay in Snow Sky or run? He had eliminated the threats posed by both Polly and Oliver Byers, but he had been caught at the newspaper office. Had the man seen his face? He wasn't sure. Lybrand had caught a glimpse of the other fellow, and he looked familiar—but many faces in this town were familiar to him.

He wondered how long it would be until Byers' body was found, and if there would be any way his death could be traced back to him. Probably not, now that he had the packet. But something had fallen out of it when the man at the *Argus* office grabbed at him. Lybrand had seen it happen but had been unable to recover the item. What if it was incriminating? The other contents of the packet scared Lybrand to death; he had no idea so much damning information about his past could be dug up by a mere Chicago newspaper reporter. He also had found Dutch Polly Coots' note to Byers in the packet; seeing it had taken away any hint of regret he had felt about killing her.

Suddenly he realized what day this was: Sunday. In a little while he would be expected to deliver a sermon. He had nothing prepared—not that he couldn't pull something from the air. He was a good improvisor.

But what if the law was looking for him? If somehow they had the goods on him? After having seen Byers' packet, he no longer could be sure that what he thought was secret really was. What if Byers had already talked to someone? What if Polly had?

That settled it. He would leave. Couldn't chance staying around to be arrested right in his pulpit. He went to his closet, flung open the door so roughly he jostled and hurt his injured hand, and got down a pair of canvas trousers and a rough cotton shirt. He would need stouter clothing than his preachery town garb when he traveled. He changed clothes, then went to his bureau and began unloading the drawers.

As he did so, the loose curtain rod Polly had pulled

down in her final struggles fell again of its own accord. The rod clattered against the floor, startling Lybrand so much he yelled. He took a breath in relief when he realized what it was, and walked across the room to replace it, for he did not want to be observed from outside.

As he lifted the wooden rod back into place, he looked out. Down the slope a lone man loped past, stopping to stare up at the cabin. Lybrand's tumultuous mind for half a moment overruled his eyes and he actually saw the figure as P. D. Viola. But Lybrand did not believe in ghosts any more than he believed in the religion he pretended to teach. It was not Viola below, but the man who had come to the door shortly before Polly had died.

Lybrand could not remember if the man had told him his name. Why was he out there, and why was he looking up here?

Suddenly his memory completed itself—not only was this the same man who had come to the door yesterday, it also was the man whom he had fought with in the *Argus* office in the night, the one he had only just now been struggling to identify.

Lybrand's hands trembled. He went to his bedside table and got his derringer, which he placed in his pocket. He had a larger pistol, a Remington, but it had been damaged and he had not bothered yet to have it fixed. Now he wished he had.

He went back to the window and looked around the curtain. There was no one below. The man had gone.

Lybrand spent the next ten minutes hurriedly finishing his preparations, then put on his hat and went out his back door. Suddenly he remembered the packet he had taken from the *Argus* office. He had not had time to destroy it. Not wanting to leave it around, Lybrand went back inside, picked up the packet from the bureau top, and went out again.

"Hello, Preacher," a breathless Abel Patterson said, stepping around the back corner. "Would have been up to see you quicker, but I had to run back to my room to get my pistol. They won't let you keep them on you in town, you know."

For a moment, Lybrand knew what sheer panic was. He backed up against his door, eyes big as dollars.

"What's the matter, Preacher? I scare you?"

Lybrand forced himself back into control. His eyes flicked down; this man indeed did have a pistol, but it was holstered—though the thong was loosened so the weapon could be quickly drawn.

"Is there something I can do for you?" Lybrand asked. "I'm in a rush at the moment."

"I'll bet you are. I'll bet you're hurrying to get out of town before they find that newspaperman's body yonder in his house. I'll bet you're hoping he didn't tell anybody else about you putting a knife into him—and about you confessing to him that you killed that poor dead woman they pulled out of the creek."

Lybrand forced a laugh. "You're insane!" he said. "I don't know what you're talking about. Who are you?"

"Don't you remember? We've met twice, once at your front door, once in the *Argus* office. You dropped this, by the way." He pulled the photograph from his pocket and tossed it at Lybrand's feet.

"Look, I don't know what you're trying to do here—"

"I'm here to bring your judgment day, Lybrand. I'm here to call you killer and deal with you for it."

"You're mad!"

"You bet I am. As mad as hell is hot. I looked at a dead woman just a little while ago and saw the face of a woman I came to this town to find. That little boy I came looking for at your door, he needs a home, and I came to give him one with my sister. I hadn't kept up with her like I should—you know how that goes. But I did write her a little and she wrote to me, telling all about her happy little family, her good life. Last I heard from her she was moving to Snow Sky. Husband was going to run a big store and they were going to live in a big house and be happier than ever. I was glad for her, Preacher. She had the good things I missed out on. At least, that's what I thought. It appears she lied to me about all that, because when I saw her lying dead beside that creek this morning they told me she was just a whore. No loss, somebody said. No loss. A woman's murdered and they say it's no loss."

Lybrand was so amazed he almost forgot his own desperate situation. "You're Polly Coots' brother?"

"She was always Polly Patterson to me. Still signed her letters that way, even after she got married—or claimed she had. Did she ever really have a husband, preacher?"

"Look, this is crazy. I—"

"Answer me!"

"She had a man at one time, I'm told. His name was Coots. She bore his child, and later he ran out on her. Took the child." Lybrand backed away half a step. "But that's just what I hear. I've never met Polly Coots.

And I'm told she died from accidental drowning, not murder."

"You're a liar. You confessed to the newspaperman that you killed her."

Lybrand felt new panic. "But Oliver Byers is..."

"Dead? Yes, he is now. But he wasn't when I found him crawling out of his house last night, bleeding like the devil. He lived long enough to tell me you're the one who cut him up—not to mention that you're also the one who beat that Viola fellow to death and killed Polly. God above, you killed my sister! Scum like you killed my brother in Chicago. I know all about you and your ilk, Lybrand, and I intend to see you go to your death for what you did. I don't know if they'll be able to convict you for Polly's death, but it doesn't matter to me what name's at the top of the case sheet. You can die for killing the preacher, the newspaperman, any of them—to me it will be Polly you're dying for. I'm ready to testify to what Byers told me."

Lybrand backed off again. "No," he said. Secretly he sneaked one hand into a pocket.

Patterson touched the butt of his pistol. "Give it up, Lybrand."

"No!" Lybrand pulled his hand from his pocket. In it was the derringer. He fired, point-blank, at Patterson's head.

"Spencer? Wait! Spencer!"

Cochran had seen a flash of color through the gaps in the wall of a nearby shed. He was far from the main part of town now, among the mines, having left the marshal's office to continue searching for Spencer. Before he had left, Cochran had conveyed Patterson's message about the dead newspaperman to Cobb, and Heck Carpenter had been sent to investigate. Cochran had not hung around to wait for the results.

"Mister?" It was a boy's voice. "Is that you?"

"I'm Tudor Cochran. You stayed at my inn on the way to Snow Sky. Do you remember?"

Spencer stepped out. He looked small, damp, frail in the sunlight. "I remember. I remember the lady there with the nice face."

Cochran knelt to bring himself more down to the boy's level. "She does have a nice face, doesn't she? That's my wife, Spencer. She cares a lot about boys like you. She worried for you and sent me after you."

"I know."

"Did your friend Mr. Patterson tell you?"

"No. I heard you say it that night outside that big tent with the music. And he's not my friend, not really."

Cochran had to think back to understand. He remembered the Dixie Lee Dance Hall, where Patterson had jumped him, and where he had described Flory's concern about the boy.

"You heard that? Where were you?"

"In the woods. I followed Mr. Patterson out."

To Spencer, Cochran's eyes looked small and glittery beneath his spectacle lenses. "We've been worried about you, Spencer. Mr. Patterson and I."

"He wants to be my father. I don't want him to be. I had to run away from him."

Cochran said, "I understand. But he cares about you, you know. He's told me that."

"But I don't want him." He paused. "I want the

lady with the nice face. I want her to be my mother, because she cared enough about me to send you."

Something in that made Cochran swallow hard. He thought of the times early in marriage when he and Flory had talked about the children they would have—and how as the years passed such talk had faded along with hope.

Cochran wanted to tell Spencer that he was going to see his wish fulfilled, but he feared that if he did, the boy would just think it was a ruse to lure him back to town and Patterson. So he merely said, "Spencer, I think you are going to find yourself a very happy boy soon. I can't tell you all about it here, but I want you to trust me, and come back with me. It's all going to be all right. I promise."

Spencer seemed to relent, but then pulled back again. "I'm scared to go back to Snow Sky," he said. "There is a really bad man there."

"I don't understand."

"A bad man. He killed a woman and put her into an outhouse over the creek, and made it fall in. I know, because I saw him do it—last night."

Cochran was stunned by this information, delivered in such a matter-of-fact way. He reached out his hand.

"Spencer, now I know you've got to come back with me. There is a man you must meet; his name is Earl Cobb. He's a good man, and he needs to hear what you just told me."

Spencer hesitated only a moment, then came forward and took Cochran's hand. Together they walked back toward the town.

Chapter 13

Lybrand rounded the rear of the Rose and Thorn and stopped to catch his breath. He had run a winding, hidden route from behind his cabin, where the man named Patterson now lay crumpled on the muddy ground. The fugitive preacher was in a panic, desperate to get out of Snow Sky but unsure of the best way to do so.

He needed a horse. On foot he could easily be followed and run down. Even though Patterson had been dealt with, Lybrand feared he ultimately would be pursued by someone else.

A jumble of voices... Lybrand edged up to the front of the alley to see where the noise was coming from. He saw a group of men, all very excited, slogging rapidly up the muddy street. At their lead was Heck Carpenter, the deputy. The group passed, agitated voices still mingling. Lybrand caught the eye of a little boy on the fringe of the group and called him over.

"What's happened?"

"Dead man found!" the boy said. "Oliver Byers, from the newspaper. Somebody stabbed him to death." The boy, unashamedly thrilled by all the excitement, rejoined the group of men on a run. They were heading for the marshal's office, Lybrand figured.

Got to find a horse, and quick, Lybrand thought. He walked back around to the rear of the Rose and Thorn and looked up the hill toward the cluster of miners' cabins standing there. Orv and Kimmie Brown's place was on the far side of that hill—and Orv had several good riding horses. One of those would do nicely. Lybrand took off at a trot.

———————◆◆————————

Cobb, seated in a chair in front of his desk, made a face as Walt Chambers bound up his ankle. "What are you trying to do—squeeze it off?" he complained.

"You nearly broke your dang ankle bone, and this won't do you no good unless it's tight," Chambers said irritably. Cobb had griped about everything Chambers had done to him in the last several minutes, and the horse doctor was tired of it.

"Won't do me no good when my foot rots off from lack of circulation, neither," Cobb said. At that moment the door opened and Tudor Cochran walked in with Spencer Vestal beside him.

"Well, hello there, gentlemen!" Cobb said. "Come here and meet our local medicine man, Walt Chambers— 'cept I'm giving him a new first name: Torture. Torture Chambers." He laughed, but not for long; his bruised ribs, now bound up tight as his foot, throbbed too badly.

Cochran was serious; he did not laugh. "Marshal, this is Spencer Vestal. He's a . . . Well, it's a long story. Just say he's a young friend of mine. He told me something a few minutes ago that was quite disturbing. It seems he may have witnessed a murder last night—the woman in the creek."

"Witnessed it?" Cobb sat up straighter, too quickly, bringing another jab of pain. "That right, son?"

Spencer, nervous and shy, nodded. He stood close to Cochran.

"Who did you see committing this murder, son?"

"I don't know his name," the boy said. "But he lives in a cabin up the hill behind that church tent. He was beating a woman."

"Exactly which cabin was it, Spencer?"

"That one sort of off by itself, almost to the top of the hill. There's a big tree down from it and I hid under it when the storm started."

"Merciful heaven, that would be the preacher's place!" Chambers exclaimed.

"So it would," Cobb said. "Spencer, did you see clear the man who did it? Was he young, old, fat, thin . . . ?"

"Young," answered Spencer, who judged age relative to his late father, older than most fathers of boys Spencer's age. "Thin. . . . He carried the woman out and put her in that outhouse. Then he made it fall in the creek."

"That's for sure Jason Lybrand," Cobb said. "Wouldn't you know it! I've had a bad feeling about that fellow from the first day he showed up here."

"Well, I for one don't believe it," Chambers said. "He's a preacher, for landsake."

At that point they were distracted by the rising noise of a small mob approaching the office. Chambers went to the door and opened it; Heck Carpenter came bursting in, several other men following.

"Earl, it's true! We found Oliver Byers dead on his bed."

"Sweet Jehosophat! What's happening to this town?" Cobb exclaimed. "Dead preachers, dead crib girls, dead newspaper editors, even a dead deputy."

"What do you want us to do?" Carpenter asked.

Cobb lifted his hand for silence and turned to Cochran. "Mr. Cochran, I believe I need a few answers from you. That man who helped you get me back here, the one who told you Byers was dead—who is he?"

Cochran knew the time for covering up was over. Enough lies had been told, and he was weary of them. "His name is Abel Patterson. He's a former Pinkerton agent from Chicago, and I came to Snow Sky following him."

"Following him? He's a friend of yours?"

"I rather feel like he is now, or might be . . . but when I followed him it was because of Spencer here. Spencer has been in the care of Patterson. The pair of them spent the night at my inn, and Flory—that's my wife—got one of her feelings about them. She thought the boy was in danger or something, so I followed them to Snow Sky to make sure he wasn't. Hiram and I—" He stopped, reddening, realizing the slip he had just made.

But Cobb didn't seem surprised. "Hiram? Hiram

Frogg, I presume—the man you keep telling me is not your friend?"

Cochran stammered, then confessed. "I lied to you, Marshal. Yes, Hiram is a friend of mine, and we rode in together. I lied because I knew he did not kill P. D. Viola, and I had to be free of suspicion myself in order to prove it."

Carpenter was becoming edgy. "Earl, shouldn't we be—"

"Hush up, Heck. I have a feeling I need to know this before we do anything. In fact, why don't you take your gaggle of goosebeckers there and wait out on the porch. You too, Walt. I'll pay you when I can."

"I've heard that before," Chambers muttered.

Carpenter gave a sour look but complied with Cobb's order. When the door was closed, Cobb said, "Let's get back on track. How did Patterson know Byers was dead?"

"He told me he found him. You see, we were out searching together for Spencer last night—Spencer had run away—and he must have run across him."

"Did you notice there was blood on Patterson's shirt?"

"Yes."

"Think he might have killed Byers?"

Cochran hadn't had time to think about it, but now that he did, it seemed possible. "Well . . . I'd hate to think of it. The truth is, though, that Byers is the one who told me most of what I know about Mr. Patterson. Byers had recognized him, knew of him back in Chicago, he said, and also saw me following Patterson around. He came asking what my interest in him was. And he said—" Cochran stopped, not really wanting to say much more.

"Go on."

"He said that Patterson came to Snow Sky with fifty thousand dollars in cash."

"That's a heck of a lot of money to be carting into a mining town. Where did he get it?"

"I don't know. Byers didn't know. I never asked Patterson about it. Our contact has been very limited—most of the time I've spent around him was last night, looking for Spencer."

"I know where the money came from," Spencer said. He had been so quiet the men had almost forgotten he was there.

"Then by all means, son, tell us," Cobb said. The man leaned over in his chair—slowly, given his hurt ribs—and smiled at Spencer to make the boy feel more at ease.

"That was money Mr. Patterson had with him when he found me," Spencer said. "He was bringing it to my father."

"Why?"

"My pap knew something bad about a rich man, and the money was from the rich man to pay Pap to keep it a secret."

"And Mr. Patterson was the delivery man, then."

"Yes."

"So why does he still have the money?"

"Because Pap died. Died right before Mr. Patterson came with the money."

"I'm sorry, son. I lost my own father, and I know it hurts."

"Not me. Pap was bad. He beat me."

A moment of silence. Hiram Frogg, oblivious to all that was going on, coughed back in his cell. Cobb said, "Are you telling me that Mr. Patterson decided to keep the money that was supposed to go to your pap?"

"Yes."

"And he kept you, too?"

"Yes."

"Why did he bring you and the money to Snow Sky?"

Spencer said, "He was bringing me to give me to his sister. Said she would give me a home. But when we got here we couldn't find her."

Cobb turned to Cochran. "Mull this over, Cochran— Oliver Byers goes to Patterson and starts talking about writing him up in the *Argus*, him and his fifty thousand dollars. If Patterson wanted to keep that quiet, which he would under the circumstances, what might he do to Byers?"

"I suppose he might kill him to keep him quiet," Cochran said. "But if he did, why did he tell me about the body? Why didn't he just keep quiet and not link himself to the situation?"

"I can't answer that. Perhaps Mr. Patterson has something the average criminal doesn't. The fact he didn't just abandon young Spencer here is evidence of it."

"What?"

"A conscience. Maybe Patterson killed Byers in a rage and after he had cooled down felt compelled to tell about the death. I've seen that sort of thing before."

"Or simpler than that," Cochran said, "maybe he didn't kill Byers at all. Sometimes people are innocent when they look guilty—like Hiram Frogg."

"Or guilty when they look innocent, like Jason Lybrand. Speaking of whom . . ." Cobb twisted his neck and yelled toward the door. "Heck! Get in here!"

The deputy, still looking irritated at having been run out by his own boss, came inside.

"I want you to deputize some men and go bring in the preacher Lybrand. We got a young fellow here who says he witnessed Lybrand committing a murder."

Carpenter, stunned to hear the preacher connected with murder, bugged out his eyes so he looked somewhat like Hiram Frogg, said his yes sir, and started to turn away. He was still too irritated at being sent out onto the porch to lower himself to ask for an explanation from Cobb.

"Wait, one more thing," Cobb said. "Did I see Fred Apple out there?"

"Yep."

"Call him in."

Apple was the town postmaster. If he hadn't held that job Cobb would have liked to have had him as a deputy, for Apple had once been a policeman in Missouri. Experienced help was hard to come by in a Colorado mining town.

"What do you need, Earl?"

"I want to make you temporary deputy and head of a posse, Fred," Cobb answered. "Got a man you need to search for."

"Wait a minute," Carpenter said. "I thought you wanted me to head the search."

"You're looking for Lybrand, Heck. He might have killed Polly Coots. I want Fred to look for a man named Abel Patterson. He might have been the one who killed

Oliver Byers. Of course, if the wrong posse brings in the right man, or however you'd say it, I won't fuss.

"We all know Lybrand. Patterson is a tall fellow, trimmed beard, blood on his shirt last time I saw him. Consider that he's likely dangerous. I want both of you to deputize as big a posse as you need, and I'd make it a fairly big one, if I was you. And Cochran, I want you to be part of Fred's posse. You know Patterson and Fred doesn't."

Cochran had never been asked to be on a posse before. "I don't have a pistol on me," he said.

"Good for you, in that you'd be in violation of the town ordinance if you did. You can borrow something from me. Fred, go out and start gathering men, quick as you can. I suggest you group up right outside here. Blast this busted-up body of mine—I wish I could go myself."

"What about Spencer?" Cochran asked.

Cobb smiled at the boy. "You pretty good at checkers, son?"

"Don't know how."

"Then you're about to be taught by a wore-out, out-of-practice master. The set's in that desk drawer there. Move it back in my bedroom—I got a bad need to lie down."

Lybrand crept around the corner of Orv Brown's horse shed, his eye on a shave-tailed beauty that looked like it could run. Lybrand had never been much of a horseman, but had enough of an eye to know a decent mount from a poor one.

"Easy, girl," he cooed, slipping toward the horse with one eye on the Brown cabin. "Easy now . . . easy . . ."

He stepped in fresh mud and slid. Instinctively he reached for the shed door, which was standing ajar, to keep from falling, and as he did made a loud thumping sound against it. The horses moved and whickered.

"Who's there?" It was Orv Brown's voice, coming from the cabin. Lybrand ran around the other side of the shed and hugged the wall. His glass-cut hand throbbed and still leaked a little blood. "Somebody up there?"

Lybrand figured that as long as he stayed quiet, Brown would take a look around and head back inside. But a moment later the cabin door thumped shut. Lybrand heard Kimmie's voice. "Orv, you're not in shape to be up—"

"Got to see what's spooking the horses, Kimmie. I'll not be robbed again."

Lybrand heard the door open and shut, and Brown's approach. Stubborn fool, that Orv Brown, Lybrand thought. He's his own worst enemy. Lybrand placed Brown's location by sound, crept around toward the front of the shed, heard the creak of the pen gate . . .

Twenty seconds passed; Lybrand heard Brown slog through the mud, step by step, closer, closer . . . Lybrand wheeled around, cleared the corner, and drove his good fist right into Brown's nose. Brown grunted, flung out his arms, and fell. Lybrand deftly caught the rifle before Brown hit the ground.

Brown, his face red with gushing blood, looked up. "Preacher?" Lybrand hit the bandaged man with the rifle butt, knocking him cold as Kimmie's scream came piercing out of the house. She had seen it all from a window.

Kimmie . . . now, there was an idea! Lybrand headed down, opened the gate, and ran onto the porch. Kimmie slammed the door shut just as he got there, but he pounded the latch open before she could lock it and threw his weight against the door, bursting it open and knocking Kimmie to the floor. Lybrand aimed the rifle at her. Kimmie's toddler daughter came around from the kitchen, saw her mother on the floor, and began to cry, not understanding what was happening but sensing something was wrong.

"Hello, Kimmie. Get up from there—you and I are going for a ride."

"My God, Reverend Lybrand—why are you doing this? Why did you hurt Orv?"

"Shut up. Get up from there and out of here—we got horses to saddle. You got two saddles?"

"Yes—"

"Good. Get moving."

"The baby . . ."

"Forget the baby. She'll be found soon enough, safe and sound, I'm sure. I need you. Protection, you know, if things get sticky. And later, other things." He smiled.

Kimmie did not know why this was happening, but it was clear that Lybrand was in some desperate situation—and also clear that he was not what she had thought he was.

Lybrand scouted around the house and found Brown's pistol and belt. He had been too disconcerted to think of taking Patterson's after he shot him. He loaded the pistol and strapped it on, and dumped extra shells into his pocket. "Come on," he ordered.

A few minutes later, Kimmie was mounted on one horse, her hands bound to the saddle horn, and Lybrand was on another. He walked his horse out of the pen, and led Kimmie's.

"We're going into the mountains," he said. "They'll check the main roads first, figuring I'll go that way for speed. But we'll be up around the Molly Bee Pass, hooking up with a couple of partners of mine."

Keeping away from town and the outlying populated areas, they circled back toward the base of the trail that led to the Molly Bee Pass. As they rode, Kimmie bowed her head and refused to let tears come, even though the fading cries of her abandoned daughter tore at her heart.

The old man at the livery stable crammed a near-handful of tobacco into his cheek; his jaw bulged out as the wad settled naturally into his fist-sized pocket that had formed over years of chewing. He leaned back against a stall door and watched the bearded man who was rather hurriedly saddling his horse.

"Pardon me," the old man said as the other tightened the cinch, "but did you know you have a right smart furrow plowed along the side of your head?"

"I was aware of it," Patterson answered.

"Looks like a bullet done it." He leaned over and launched a coffee-colored stream from his mouth. "You been in a fight of some kind?"

"Now you've gone to meddling," Patterson said in a friendly tone.

"Got blood down your shirt, too. I'd say you was running from the law, if I had to guess."

"You don't have to."

"Don't you worry none about me—I run from the law plenty myself in my younger days. Did you know I holed up with Jesse James one night? Down in Tennessee he was at that time. And I rid for a week with Simon Caine during the hostilities. Hard as nails, Caine was. Yes sir, I was a wild buck in my young days. Man running from the law's got nothing to fear from me. My lip's sewed tight when law comes looking."

"I'm not running from the law, if it makes any difference," Patterson said. "Not that I know of, at least. But I'm looking for a fellow who is, or will be."

"He give you that gully in your head?"

"Sure did. He assumed he had killed me, I think. Knocked me clean out for a few minutes, but I'm still kicking."

Patterson dug money from his pocket. "Keep the change—if you'll tell me the way a man on the run would most likely leave Snow Sky."

"Well sir, there's any number of ways out. You could take the main road if you wanted to go fast, or any of these mountain trails if you wanted to hide in the hills."

"Any of those mountain trails connect with main roads farther on?"

"None but the trail through the Molly Bee."

"Where's that?"

"Yonder way." The man pointed. "Go out back, cross the creek, and take the road between them two hills you'll see." The old man put on a devilish grin. "My compadres and me calls them hills Molly Bee's breasts." He cackled. "Yes sir, that's what we call 'em, no fooling!"

"Clever bunch, you and your compadres," Patterson said. He wiped away the last of the blood exuding from his head wound; the rest had scabbed to a crust. He then led his horse out the big double back door of the livery, just as another man came running in the front. He was a boyish version of the older fellow.

"Papaw, they's two posses forming down at the marshal's office!" the young man said. "They's looking for the preacher Lybrand and for another fellow too. The preacher Lybrand, they say he kilt Dutch Polly Coots, and the other fellow kilt the man running the newspaper. I going to get me my rifle and go down and—" The flood of words stopped as the speaker noticed Patterson. "Papaw—that there looks like he might be the fellow one of them posses is after."

The old man pivoted his hoary head toward Patterson. "You told me there wasn't no law after you!"

"Didn't know there was," Patterson said as he drew his pistol. "I suppose I ought to ask you to open that stall door."

The old man spat. "Reckon you orta." He opened the stall and stepped inside. "Come on, Dwayne." He pronounced it Dee-wayne. "He'll want you in here too."

"If'n I had my pistol I'd take him to the law," the younger man said as he stepped inside.

"Good thing for me and you that you didn't," Patterson responded. He closed the door, wedged it shut with a long board jammed up against another stall on the far side, and then tied a rope across the door to keep it from opening even if the board was knocked free. "That ought to hold you awhile," Patterson said.

"It orta."

Patterson mounted and headed for the trail up to the Molly Bee. When he reached the twin hills the old man had chortled about, he saw fresh horse prints in the muddy trail. Two horses, traveling fast. He hoped one of them carried Lybrand. Perhaps the second was a spare mount.

No way to be sure if Lybrand had come this way, but his intuitions felt right, and at the moment that was all he had to go on. He passed between the hills and continued up the trail.

Chapter 14

The air became cooler and thinner the higher they went. Kimmie Brown shivered uncontrollably, but it wasn't from the cold. She felt doomed, and every lurching, upward step of her horse made her husband and deserted child seem more distant. For all she knew, Orv was dead; she had not even been given the chance to check before Lybrand stole her away.

She could hardly believe the roughly dressed, profane man who held her hostage was the same polite gentleman she had seen behind the pulpit so many Sundays past. She wondered if he had gone insane . . . or if she had.

Her horse stumbled and she almost fell from the saddle. The ropes binding her hands to the saddle horn tore at her wrists. Lybrand twisted in the saddle, glared at her, and swore. He stopped, dismounted, and pushed her back into the saddle. She kicked at him.

Lybrand drew his stolen pistol and stuck it under her chin. Slowly he clicked back the hammer.

"It would be ironic for you to die from a bullet fired by your own husband's pistol, wouldn't it? Come now, Kimmie—it needn't be this way. You can enjoy your life with me, I assure you . . . or you can throw your life away if you refuse to cooperate. You decide."

She glared at him, still refusing to give in to tears.

"Don't think I'd hesitate to get rid of you, Kimmie, no matter how I feel about you. I've killed three people already this week, and I don't have much to lose by adding a fourth. But I don't want to kill you. I care about you, Kimmie. I always have. I used to look at you from the pulpit, think about you. Could you feel it? You could, I know you could."

She shuddered. His talk made her feel sick.

Lybrand tried to read her expression. "Worrying over your family? Don't. I didn't kill your husband. He'll live to take care of your child. Forget them. You're with me now."

"Orv will come after you. He won't stop until you're dead."

"No fool worse than a stubborn fool. If he follows, I'll deal with him later."

Lybrand thumbed down the hammer and holstered the pistol. He remounted.

Cochran wasn't sure how to feel about riding in a posse, particularly one searching for Abel Patterson. While looking for Spencer last night along with Patterson, Cochran had come to like the ex-Pinkerton. It was hard now to picture Patterson as a potential murderer, despite the convincing case Cobb had outlined. And Cochran knew firsthand that Byers had been the aggravating sort who easily could drive someone to kill him in anger.

Posses, Cochran had assumed, were fast-moving, powerful bands that swept the land like righteous angels bringing in wrongdoers. But Apple's posse just sort of plodded along. No one had any idea where to look for Patterson, or even if he was in town. Only Cochran knew first-hand what Patterson looked like.

Apple rode beside Cochran at the head of the ten-man party. The riders wound through town, looking about, asking questions of people on the street, all in all seeming to Cochran like a rather ineffective force.

At length they wound up outside town, riding up the road that led toward the Cochran Inn, a day and a half away. "Maybe we'll meet somebody coming in who might have seen Patterson going out—if he went this way," Apple said.

It seemed to Cochran that finding Patterson like this was about as likely as shooting a crow through the head by firing blindfolded at the sky. But he kept his peace; Apple was the one with law experience, not he.

Two miles out of town, Apple raised his hand and stopped the posse. "Take a look." He nodded forward.

Two riders were coming toward them. Both wore dusters, big-brimmed hats, and broad mustaches. From the looks of them they had been on the trail quite a long time.

Apple waited for them to approach. When they were twenty feet away they stopped. Both touched their hats as one.

"Gentlemen," Apple said.

"Good day, sir," one of the pair returned. He cast a

glance across the group. "This has the look of an official party."

"A posse. Looking for a man name of Abel Patterson. You see anybody come out this way?"

The men glanced at each other. "No sir," the first man said.

"You're sure?"

"Had we seen Abel Patterson, I assure you we would know it. We're looking for him too." The man reached beneath his duster and pulled out a folding wallet. He opened it, rode up a few feet, and handed it to Abel. "My credentials. I'm J. B. Fulton, Pinkerton agent. My partner here is Ken Lambertson. Also affiliated with Pinkerton."

"Pinkertons! Why are you looking for Patterson?"

"We'll be glad to answer that—if you will do the same."

Apple glanced at Cochran and shrugged. "No harm in that, I guess." Then to Fulton: "He's suspected in the murder of a local newspaperman. Somebody stabbed the fellow to death."

Fulton shook his head. "It wasn't Patterson. I know him too well. Under no circumstances would he murder a man. If he's killed anyone, it's in self-defense."

"How do you know him so well?"

"Used to work with him. And as I said, we've been sent after him. He took a bad turn. A very wealthy fellow is alleging that Patterson took a large sum of money that belonged to him. Some sort of payment—extortion, I figure—that Patterson was to deliver. Our man got wind the fellow who was to receive the money died before it ever came—but Patterson never brought back the money. We were hired to find him, and a hard trail it's been, I'll tell you. Patterson knows how to cover his tracks. He was good when I worked with him, and he's good now."

Apple asked, "You gentlemen interested in joining our search party here?"

"No thanks. And I suggest you look elsewhere—Patterson has not come this way."

Apple sighed, turned to his posse, and said, "Gentlemen, let's turn it around. We're going back to Snow Sky."

Lybrand stopped when he saw the bridge over the gorge was gone. Disbelieving, he dismounted and walked, rifle in hand, to the edge of the gorge. He had all but forgotten the storm, and the possibility it could have wiped out his only way across this obstacle had never crossed his mind.

He scanned the fallen bridge, now a crumpled mass of logs and puncheons, then raised his eyes to the maze of rocks on the far, steep side. Beyond them, out of his view from here, stood the cabin in which Dade and Daugherty were holed up. If they were there, perhaps they could tell him some other way across. He cupped his hands and started to shout, then realized there could be someone trailing him. If so, he didn't want to advertise his exact location. He would have to find an alternate way across on his own—though that could only mean cutting along the length of the gorge and going back through the forest itself. That would slow him down considerably, especially with Kimmie along.

But there was one other option. They could abandon their horses, climb down in the gorge, and scale the other side. That would put them on foot, but also would have them across the gorge much more quickly. They could connect with Daugherty and Dade in the cabin and leave together. Daugherty and Dade had only one horse each, meaning Lybrand and Kimmie would have to double with them until they could steal other mounts, but that was a minor problem. The worst thing Lybrand would have to face would be the anger of his partners at having to abandon their scheme to clean out the House of Prayer bank account.

Lybrand, turning, happened to glance to his right and downward into the churning water at the base of the gorge, near the waterfall.

A body was there, half out of the water, half in, caught between two rocks sticking out from the bank. It was Ivan Dade. Breathing faster now, Lybrand scanned the rest of the area. Farther up from the waterfall he saw Daugherty's corpse, caught by the shirt collar on a protruding limb, his feet pointing downstream with the current.

Dead. Both of them dead. How? Had the bridge fallen with them on it?

He heard her behind him a second before he saw her, and when he wheeled she was already upon him, pushing him back and over the edge of the gorge. He fell, hit the slope, and rolled down it toward the water, losing his rifle along the way.

Kimmie, her wrists bleeding from having slipped the tight ropes, let out a spontaneous scream, then wheeled and ran back down the way they had come, too distraught even to think of taking one of the horses.

———————◆—◆—◆———————

Patterson heard the scream echoing back down the trail. A woman? He pieced it together: The extra set of hoofprints on the trail were not left by a spare horse, but by a second rider—apparently female.

A girlfriend? A hostage? Patterson could not know, not yet. But a few moments later he saw a pretty woman coming back down the trail. When she saw him she stopped so quickly she fell.

He dismounted and went to her. "It's all right, lady—relax. I won't hurt you." He pointed up the hill. "Lybrand?"

Kimmie was too breathless to answer, but she nodded rapidly.

"You were his hostage, maybe?"

Another fast nod.

"Where is he?"

"Knocked him . . . into a gorge . . . just up the hill."

"Here . . ." Patterson led Kimmie to his horse. "You ride on down to Snow Sky. Don't stop for anything. I'm going after Lybrand." He helped her mount, turned the horse, slapped its rump. As Kimmie rode away, he drew his pistol and headed up the slope.

Kimmie rode like she had never ridden before. Patterson's horse was swift despite weariness, particularly on this downslope. The farther she got from Lybrand, the safer she felt. Happiness began to rise. Ahead was her home, her husband, her baby.

When she came out from between the hills at the base of the trail, she careened toward town, crossed the Bledsoe Creek bridge, the horse gracefully leaping the missing portion, and sped past the livery, not noticing the crowd of men there. She was bound for home, and nothing would distract her.

"Hey—that looks to be the same horse!" the old man said, pointing after her. "That woman's riding the horse that belongs to the fellow what shut us up in the stall!"

Heck Carpenter asked, "Are you sure?"

"No doubt. Saddle's the same, too, ain't it, Dee-wayne?"

Carpenter singled out two of his men. "Go after her. See what's going on. I think that was Kimmie Brown." He turned back to the two men he had just freed from the stall. "Good thing you gents know how to holler loud. That man, was his name Patterson?"

"Don't rightly know. When he put his horse in here t'other day he used the name Johnson."

"Yeah, but when I come in talking about joining the posse, that's when he locked us up," Dwayne said. "Must have been Patterson."

"Which way did he take off?"

"Right up toward the Molly Bee."

"Let's go after him, then," Carpenter said. "If he lost his horse to Kimmie Brown somehow—and don't ask me to figure that one out—then likely he's on foot. That ought to make him easier to catch."

"Don't count on that," the old man said. "That fellow, he struck me as a slick one. And I can tell things like that. I was wild in my younger days, you know. I was with Jesse James once't."

"Tell me about it one of these days, then," Carpenter said, trying not to act impressed but in fact being very much so, for he had read a score of Jesse James dime novels. "Right now I got work to do. Forget about

Lybrand, men—we're going after Patterson. At least we know where he went." Carpenter was determined to outdo Apple, whom he knew Cobb held in higher regard.

The posse galloped off toward the Molly Bee trail. The old man and his son walked to the back of the livery and watched them head for the twin hills. "Been a sweet sort of day, ain't it, Dee-wayne?" the old man said. "Ain't had this much excitement since I rid with Simon Caine. No sir."

Patterson saw the horses first, standing where they had been left. From the horn of one of the saddles hung a curl of cord, wet with blood from Kimmie Brown's wrists. He noted that beside the other horse lay a packet that apparently had been half stuck into a saddlebag, but had fallen out. It was the packet Lybrand had taken from the *Argus*, he figured.

No Jason Lybrand in sight. Patterson saw the gorge ahead. He crept forward, pistol out, trying to be as silent as he could, hoping that any noise he might make would be masked by the sound of the waterfall. The distance to the gorge seemed infinite, every step an effort. His pulse pounded inside his temples, making the bullet furrow on his head throb.

He came to the edge of the gorge and saw Lybrand too late to duck, so he was fully exposed when Lybrand fired. Lybrand had only then regained his rifle, for he had been stunned by the roll into the gorge, and his rifle had fallen into a crevice and had been hard to find. In fact, he had literally plucked it out of the crevice, whipped it up, and fired it just as Patterson appeared. Haste made for bad aim, and he missed. Patterson backed off.

"Show yourself again and you're a dead man!" Lybrand yelled.

Patterson figured surprise was his best hope. "All right, all right . . . I'm not foolish. I'm backing away—I'll leave . . ."

With that he plunged forward, landing on his stomach at the edge of the gulch. He fired a quick shot at Lybrand. The false preacher screamed and grabbed at his shoulder. The rifle hit the ground. Blood streamed between Lybrand's fingers.

"Next one I put through your skull," Patterson said. "Give it up. Come up here with me and I'll take you back to Snow Sky."

Lybrand shook his head. "I can't go back. I'll never go back. There's too much against me there."

"You have the same right to a fair trial that any man's got. Come on—live. Don't make me kill you."

"I can't go back . . . can't." Lybrand wobbled on his feet. Even from yards away he looked increasingly weak. "Can't go back." He sank to his haunches, then sat on a rock.

Patterson said, "Scoot that rifle away. You're too close to it."

Lybrand slowly reached for the rifle—then suddenly it was in his hands, being levered. Lybrand came up, dodging to the side as Patterson fired. Lybrand fired next, and it was Patterson's turn to scream. A slug pounded through the flesh of his upper arm. He dropped his pistol and it fell into the gorge. Patterson rolled back away from the edge.

Lybrand was a good actor; he had certainly fooled

Patterson. Obviously the bullet Lybrand had taken had not harmed him as much as he had pretended. Patterson quickly examined his own wound, which was bleeding freely, but was relatively superficial. That made twice today that Lybrand had tried to kill him but had managed only to wound. Patterson doubted he would be so lucky a third time—especially without a gun to answer with.

Realizing that if Lybrand came back up the slope on this side, there would be nothing to anticipate but a quick slaughter, Patterson headed back down the trail toward Snow Sky and then on a rocky stretch cut into the forest to his left. He hoped Lybrand would not attempt to follow him, but if he did, at least he would lose all sign once he reached the rocks. In the forest Patterson edged back up toward the gorge, staying far from the trail so he wouldn't be seen should Lybrand be on it.

He saw a knoll ahead and went to it. He scrambled up it and from the top found, as he had hoped he would, that through the evergreens he could see into the gorge a little. He waited there, wondering what Lybrand would do. A few minutes later he saw him— on this side of the gorge—heading back toward the edge, carrying the packet that had been on the ground beside the horses. Lybrand must have gone back to the horses and picked it up. The young man, seemingly ignoring the wound Patterson had given him, descended into the gulch on the shallow side. After three minutes had passed, Patterson saw Lybrand climbing up the other side, moving relatively fast up the steep rock face, his rifle thrust through his belt, the packet in his teeth. Patterson had to grudgingly admire Lybrand's determination and ability to ignore pain.

A minute later, Lybrand cleared the far side of the

gorge and vanished among the rocks there. Patterson stood, slid down the rounded front of the knoll, and headed for the gorge himself, cutting straight through the forest.

He waited a few moments before coming out into the clear, for he feared Lybrand might be hidden in the rocks on the other side, waiting for him to appear. When finally Patterson did come out in the open, no gunfire greeted him. He ran forward, paused at the gorge to assess the smoothest way down, then made another slide.

He looked for his dropped pistol at the bottom but did not find it. It must have been lost in the water. He splashed through the water, which was not as high now that some of the storm runoff had drained away, and made it to the other side. He stumbled across something and was stunned to see it was a dead body... and not far away was another. Two mysteries—two he would have to ignore. Catching Lybrand was the important thing.

He scaled the wall on the other side, which was not easy, given his arm wound. Using the muscles hurt him terribly, but he would not give up. He kept seeing the face of his dead sister, kept thinking about the fact that the man who killed her was even now escaping. With a final heave, Patterson pulled himself up and immediately ran into the rocks.

There was more trail here, and it led to a cabin. The little log hut was tucked back against a low bluff. Beside it was a crude corral, the gate open. Patterson eyed the cabin until he felt reasonably confident it was empty, then went to the edge of the corral. Fresh tracks of two horses pockmarked the dirt; Lybrand had probably just now taken a horse from this corral, and either turned the other loose or trailed it along.

Patterson edged over to the cabin; the door was open. He peered in. As he had thought, no one was inside, but it was obvious someone was staying here— or had been. He remembered the bodies. Perhaps those men had lived in this place.

A glint of light on something in the corner caught his eye. A rifle! Lybrand must have overlooked it; he would not have left it behind willingly, Patterson figured. Beside the rifle, on the floor, were a box of shells and a Colt pistol.

Patterson checked the rifle—loaded. The pistol as well. He tucked the pistol behind his back, in his belt, pocketed the extra rifle shells, and walked out. Scanning the ground, he picked up hoofprints, and followed them on a run.

Once again the land began to rise, the air to become even thinner. Patterson panted as he ascended. It was easy to follow the tracks of the horses; here there was only one trail they could follow in any case. It wound up between rocks, heading toward the timberline.

Patterson stopped, leaning over with his hands on his knees, gasping. His injured arm hurt badly; so did his head. He began to lose the hope he had gained when he found the firearms. Patterson could not outperform a stout horse used to the mountains. Lybrand was going to get away after all.

The thought brought despair. Patterson remembered Polly as a young girl, a baby he had held in his arms when he was just a child himself. Too bad he had lost touch with her as much as he had. Perhaps he could have steered her off whatever course finally had made her a mining town prostitute. A sad thing Polly's life must have been.

"I'll try, Polly. Try to get him for you," Patterson said aloud. He stood and began trotting up the slope again.

As he rounded a turn, a horse stood before him, bridled but barebacked. Patterson scanned the high rocks, looking for evidence of ambush, and found none. Slowly he advanced to the horse.

The reins were bloodied. Apparently Lybrand was bleeding worse; perhaps the blood itself had made the reins slip from his hands. Probably this was the second horse, which he had led away to keep any pursuer from using it against him.

Patterson hefted himself up onto the horse and headed up the trail again. He rounded a bend, came around a monolith of stone, and knew even before he heard the shot that he had brought himself squarely into a trap.

Lybrand fired from somewhere above; the slug tore through Patterson's side, to the left of his stomach. He fell from the horse, landing on his right side. He tried to raise the rifle with his left arm, but Lybrand fired again and put a bullet through his forearm, breaking it. The rifle fell. Patterson struggled not to pass out.

Lybrand stood up behind the boulder that had hidden him. Smiling broadly, he approached. There was little blood on him; the wound he had received was obviously superficial. He must have smeared blood on the reins of the horse deliberately, to make Patterson think he was worse off than he was. Patterson had to hand it to Lybrand: the ruse had worked.

Patterson twisted, moving his right arm from beneath him, putting his hand behind him . . . and Lybrand approached, laughing now, bearing down on him as he levered his rifle again.

"Viola, Polly, Byers—and now you," Lybrand said.

Still walking, he raised the rifle to hip level, aimed it at Patterson's upper chest—and Patterson heaved up, clearing enough room between himself and the ground for his right arm to come forward, the Colt pistol in his grip.

Lybrand never got a chance to squeeze off a shot. Patterson's bullet took him in the gut, doubling him over. The next shot caught his right shoulder, kicking him back, making him stumble, screaming, toward a steep slope behind him. His arms flailed and then he was gone.

Patterson closed his eyes for a few moments. Then he opened them, made himself get up. He staggered to the edge of the slope, looked down.

Nothing. Just a barren, rocky slope, nothing on it big enough to hide a man, no vegetation into which a body might disappear—but no Jason Lybrand, either. But it seemed impossible. Even if Lybrand had been able to run away, he still would be well within view.

But he wasn't. Patterson was mystified, but the feeling gave way quickly to one of sickness. He sank to his knees, then fell forward, almost rolling down the slope himself.

Near the base of that slope, fifteen feet deep in a narrow crack in the rock that Patterson had not even been able to see from the top, Jason Lybrand lay wedged sideways, his throat crushed against a bulge of stone so tightly that he could barely get breath into his constricted lungs, yet could make no sound other than the same sort of squeaks P. D. Viola had made in his last hours. Lybrand wanted to scream for help, but could not, and even if he had, the only man who could have helped him would have been unable to do so, downed as he was by bullets Lybrand himself had fired.

The worst of it was, the pinching rock was hampering Lybrand's loss of blood from his gut wound. Eventually, he knew, he would bleed to death . . . eventually. But before that would be hours in this living hell of constriction, enclosure—the things that Lybrand had feared and hated more than anything else for as long as he could remember.

Life had seemed short so far to Jason Lybrand. But he knew that would be made up to him, for what time remained would seem long indeed.

Time passed; he heard Heck Carpenter's posse arrive, heard them exclaiming over Patterson, heard them search the area, saw their shadows pass above, heard them find the horses and the packet. He tried again and again to scream but could not. Then they were gone.

Time dragged on and torment drove Lybrand's sanity from him. He shifted his eyes upward and saw a man crouching above the crevice, looking down at him, smiling. Lybrand squeaked again and the man laughed and waved. It was P. D. Viola. Lybrand closed his eyes, and when he looked again Viola was not there.

For the rest of his life, Jason Lybrand was alone.

Chapter 15

Cochran walked up to the door of the marshal's office, knocked, then went on in. Heck Carpenter, sliding his dime novel into a drawer, nodded a hello.

"The marshal wanted to see me?" Cochran asked.

"That's right." Then, over his shoulder, "Earl! He's here!"

Cobb came out of his side room, hobbling stiffly on his crutch, making a face with each step. But he looked more rested than the last time Cochran had seen him. "How you coming along?" Cochran asked.

"Tolerably well. And what about Patterson? You seen him today?"

"Yes. Just came from there. Walt Chambers was with him, and he's optimistic. Says he'll make it, though it may be a long time before he's fit to travel."

"Them Pinkertons hanging around still?"

"Yes, just waiting on Patterson to heal up so they

212

can take him back. And Spencer stays by Patterson's side every waking hour. Funny thing how the boy has grown so close to him all at once. When he found out how hard Patterson looked for him, and how he went after Lybrand all alone, he started seeing him as a hero."

Cobb sat down slowly, then eased his crutch to the floor beside his chair. "I plan to talk to Patterson soon as he's more fit. When he gets clear of this stolen money problem he's facing, I want him to know he's got a job here if he wants it. Probably he won't—being a Snow Sky deputy don't pay a heck of a lot, and it ain't got the prestige of being a Pinkerton."

"Amen," Carpenter muttered from over at the window, where he was looking out onto the street.

"He may take you up on it in any case," Cochran said. "There's not much prestige in being an ex-Pinkerton and ex-convict, either."

"Let me get to the thing I called you here for," Cobb said. He laid his hand atop a big pile of papers on top of the desk. "Judge Worth was in town this morning, and we conducted us a quiet little hearing. The judge looked over these papers and such, the stuff that came out of the packet they found on Lybrand's horse. The packet was addressed to Oliver Byers, and came from somebody on the Chicago *Tribune*—an old friend of Byers', we gather from the letter in it. It's all about Jason Lybrand, and sheds a lot of light on that bird. Seems he had a past relationship with P. D. Viola that wasn't what he presented to us." He briefly outlined the history of Lybrand and the Viola family. "Viola wasn't coming to Snow Sky to help Lybrand build his church at all. He was coming for revenge."

"Which supports what Patterson and Kimmie Brown say about Lybrand being Viola's killer."

"It does, and the judge sees it the same way I do. We've decided there is no case to be made against Hiram Frogg. I called you over thinking you might want to be here when we let him go. I would have freed him sooner, but I wanted to see how the judge saw it."

Cochran let fly a wide grin.

"Heck, you do the honors, huh?" Cobb said.

A minute later, Frogg was standing in the office beside Cochran, beaming in the joy of freedom as he shook hands with Cobb and Heck Carpenter.

"I thought there for a bit that my time had come," Frogg said. "I figured the law would see me dead."

"You didn't kill Viola," Cobb said. "There's no doubt in my mind Lybrand is our man. Another hearing or two, and I think we can officially lay three murder charges on Lybrand's back."

"But he's not here to bear them," Cochran said.

"No. That's a puzzle, too. Don't know if Lybrand's alive or dead. Never heard of a man vanishing like that before. Maybe someday we'll know what happened. It's as if the earth itself swallowed him up.

"We'll put out notice Lybrand is wanted, but I have a feeling we'll see no results from it. I only hope there's enough justice in this world that he somehow got what was coming to him, and that Snow Sky never sees the like of him again."

Cochran and Frogg headed back to Patterson's bedside and found the man much improved. Cochran

introduced Frogg; hands were shaken. Spencer was at
Patterson's bedside, as before.

"Well, I told Cochran I'd investigate to see you
cleared, and it didn't really work out for me to do it,"
Patterson said to Frogg.

"The end result came out right for me, and you
had your part in it," Frogg said. "That's what matters."

"And what's ahead for you now, Mr. Patterson?"
Cochran asked.

"Fulton and Lambertson are hovering around like
two buzzards waiting to haul me off," Patterson answered.
"Suppose I'll do some jail time for keeping that black-
mail money." Patterson reached down and fondly ruffled
Spencer's hair; the boy grinned. "I don't look forward to
what I'll have to face, but still I'm ready for it. I'm tired
of running and worrying. I'll do my time, then after
that, who knows?"

"The marshal just informed me he'll make you
Snow Sky deputy anytime you want to be," Cochran said.

Patterson lifted his brows. "You don't say! Well, I
could give it some thought. Lord knows being locked
up will give me plenty of time to think."

"Whenever you're free, and if you come back
through here, I hope you'll stop at the inn," Cochran
said. "Free room and board for you anytime. Me and
Flory and Hiram will be glad to see you."

"I'll take you up on that. And you can bet I'll be
there. I'll want to see how this boy here is shaping up."
He scruffed his hand through Spencer's hair again.

"Well, you won't see me about the inn if you come
through," Frogg said.

Cochran turned, surprised. "What?"

"I'm staying in Snow Sky. Opening up a smithy.

Like Mr. Patterson said, being locked up gives you time to think. I thought about it, and decided that a man has to settle down sometime or another."

Cochran smiled and stuck out his hand. "Glad for it, then," he said. "I'll miss having you about, though, Hiram."

"Yeah, but think how happy Flory will be that old Toad ain't around no more. But don't worry—I'll be in to visit, and you can let me stay in that free room you offered Mr. Patterson."

Cochran gave Frogg a friendly frown and then turned to Spencer. "Son, are your feelings still the same about coming to live with Flory and me?"

"Yes," Spencer said. "If yours are."

Warm relief spread through Cochran. He had feared Spencer's newfound affection for Patterson would change his notions about whom he wanted to spend his life with—not that Patterson would have been able to take care of the boy for a long time to come, in any case.

"I still feel exactly the same way," Cochran said. "Come on. Let's let Mr. Patterson rest a bit. We'll go to the Rose and Thorn and have us a good piece of pie."

"With cream on it?" Spencer asked.

"A gallon, if you want it. You come too, Hiram."

"Sorry. I'm more in the humor for a beer."

Outside on the boardwalk, Spencer slipped his hand into Cochran's. "You called me 'son' in there," he said.

"I did. And from now on, that's what you are."

"But what if your wife doesn't want me?"

"She will. I know Flory mighty well, Spencer. You're the answer to her prayers."

Spencer looked down; Cochran could feel him shyly hiding his smile. "First thing when we get there,

I'm going to shine up these shoes," Spencer said. "They're the ones Mr. Patterson got for me, and that makes them special."

"That it does, son."

———◆———

The next day about noon, Cochran saddled his horse, listening to the talkative old liveryman drone on about his much-prized wild past, and then he bought a cheap mount and battered old saddle for Spencer. That was the best Cochran could afford at the moment.

All the way back, Spencer talked—endless chatter, a young lifetime's worth of observations, questions, feelings, too long pent up inside but now flowing like a dam had been broken.

They slept on the roadside and the next morning rode on, taking it slow, until the sunset brought them to the Cochran Inn.

Flory stood at the door, having seen them coming down the road. The ruddy glow from the west shone on her face, and Cochran watched her expression. He could tell from here that when she saw the boy she began to wonder if maybe, just maybe . . .

Cochran spurred his horse and galloped in the rest of the way. Spencer, nervous now that the moment of arrival had come, hung back and watched Cochran talking with excited expression and sweeping gestures to his wife. Her look of confusion gave way to a smile, and she turned toward Spencer and opened her arms.

The boy, alone no longer, rode into the yard of the Cochran Inn and the beginning of happiness that was not to fade.

If you enjoyed Cameron Judd's latest western novel, be sure to look for his biggest, boldest book yet—the epic story of the Tennessee frontier in the turbulent eighteenth century.

THE OVERMOUNTAIN MEN

Bantam Books is proud to publish
Cameron Judd.

Look for THE OVERMOUNTAIN MEN
wherever you buy Bantam Books.

On sale June, 1991.

Joshua Byrum knelt where slanting rays of morning sun, piercing in through the open cabin door, touched the dirt floor of the house of Awahili of Tikwalitsi. Before him lay a naked, sweat-drenched Cherokee boy, swaddled in trade blankets, and in the boy's left hand was a wing feather of a hawk.

In Awahili's house this breezy Sunday morning, October 19, 1760, the smell of illness was almost as strong as that of the heavy woodsmoke rising toward the roof hole from the dying central fire. Joshua had wrinkled his nose at the sickly stench the moment he had ducked inside the door. Now he looked around the cabin, letting his eyes recover from the brilliant autumn sun outside and adjust to the dimmer interior light. He squeezed the crude rawhide grip of his flint knife tightly, swallowed with a sandy throat, and wondered if he would have either the opportunity or the courage to do what he had come to do.

At the moment all was relatively quiet in the Cherokee village of Tikwalitsi, the pervading stillness being broken only by barking dogs, windborne voices, rustling trees, and the steady, distant thump of a squaw's wood pestle in a corn mortar hollowed from a hickory log. Ten-year-old Joshua had sneaked through the town's mix of log summer houses, earth-covered winter hot-houses, corncribs, food shelters, and gardens filled with dead vines and brown stalks, and settled in a hidden place to watch the house where lived Awahili, known to the white men as the Bloody Eagle of Tikwalitsi. Only when he saw the warrior's wife leave to gather firewood by the river did he go to the cabin and enter.

No one had seen him, and he had not expected that anyone would. Joshua was proudly aware of his inborn ability to travel silently and unseen, and on this, his chosen day of vengeance, the skill had served him well.

But now he was bewildered. He had heard talk of sickness in the house of Bloody Eagle, and it had been his understanding that it was the warrior himself who was ill. Seemingly that was not true, for Bloody Eagle was not here. Joshua wondered if the warrior might be in his winter house, trying to sweat away his illness, but a glance outside revealed no smoke rising from the conical winter house. Obviously it was this boy, not Bloody Eagle himself, who was ill, and Joshua had simply misunderstood.

Joshua looked closely at the sleeping Indian's face. The youth's thick hair and smooth brow were sodden. Despite his dark, almost olive skin, the Cherokee looked wan and wasted, and each breath obviously required effort. He trembled slightly as he slept; the tremors evidenced themselves in the shaking of the hawk's feather held against his chest. Joshua wondered if the feather had medical or spiritual significance, for he knew the Cherokees' respect for the great Tlanuwas. Those mighty hawks of legend, the storytellers said, had destroyed a serpentine, water-dwelling Uktena, a fearsome creature in which even the white traders firmly believed. Maybe the feather made reference to them for some reason—or maybe it had simply blown in the door and the sick boy had picked it up idly or unconsciously in his writhings.

Joshua felt an unexpected surge of pity, and was displeased. Over these past many weeks he had striven to erase such soft feelings. If he yielded to them, he feared, they would render him unable to do the grim task he felt was his duty, the task he had come there to do. But Joshua's pity for the boy, whom he now recognized as the orphaned nephew of Bloody Eagle, the only son of the pox-scarred warrior's sister, would not subside. Joshua grew angry with himself.

That a kinsman of Bloody Eagle, of all men, should so affect him was intolerable. Joshua had much cause to hate Bloody Eagle. That warrior, in conjunction with the great chief Oconostota, had been a main instigator of the recent long siege of Fort Loudoun. Because of that siege, Joshua had suffered much, and lost much, and he would not forget or forgive it.

Joshua turned to see the familiar scalplock that hung on a post outside Bloody Eagle's door, and let the dried clump of flesh and windblown hair restir his hatred. He looked down at the knife he had secretly chipped out over the past month from a long shard of flint, and mentally repeated the vow he had made a few weeks before on a bloody massacre field as a jubilant Bloody Eagle tauntingly slapped in his face that same gruesome scalp that now stirred in the wind outside. He had sworn that he would similarly slay and scalp Bloody Eagle, even at the cost of his own life. Since then he had repeated the vow to himself until he had lost all doubt he could fulfill it.

Now, though, Joshua was not so confident. Bloody Eagle's unexpected absence threw matters out of balance. If I'm wise, Joshua thought, I will leave and await another opportunity.

The idea seemed temptingly sensible, yet Joshua was reluctant to follow it. It had taken too long to build up his courage to make even this attempt; he doubted he would be able to do so again.

Then a new possibility suddenly came to mind. He could achieve his vengeance even with Bloody Eagle absent. After all, would not the best revenge be to slay the son of the warrior's sister, the youth whom under Cherokee practice it was the responsibility of Bloody Eagle, as maternal uncle, to discipline and train as a warrior?

The thought made Joshua's heart race. Fighting away his lingering sense of pity, he lifted the stone blade high and held it in both hands. For several moments he was gripped by a strange paralysis and could not move or breathe, but with a great forcing of his will finally brought down the knife.

At the last second he faltered, averting the blade to the side. The flint blade stuck into the dirt floor and snapped at the center. At the same time, the long-straining wall shoring up Joshua's emotions also broke, and against his will he began to cry. Now he did not feel at all like the brave and vengeful man he had wanted to be, but instead like the frightened captive child he truly was. The idea of more revenge and violence no longer held any appeal. He had seen more than enough of both these past months.

Ashamed of his crying, Joshua quickly dried his tears on the sleeve of his homespun shirt. Picking up the pieces of his knife, he tucked them inside the pocket formed by the shirt itself where it draped over the cloth sash around his thin waist. When he looked again at the Indian boy, he was surprised to see the sunken eyes tremble open, and the face turn toward him. The Cherokee initially stared listlessly at Joshua, then looked afraid as he realized this was a stranger, and a white one at that.

For many moments the two boys looked at each other in silence, each fearing the other. Finally Joshua lifted his head haughtily and tried to sound gruff and manly when he spoke.

"I am Ayunini, the swimmer," he said, slapping his right hand across his chest. "I am very brave and strong."

Joshua was proud of the Cherokee name by which Attakullakulla, whom the whites called the Little Carpenter, had called him. Using it made Joshua feel more courageous, and more a part of the world in which he was now forced to live.

Though his status as a prisoner within the Cherokees' world was new to him, that world itself was not. He had lived among the Overhill Cherokees for three years, since he and his mother had accompanied his father and Henry Dorey across the mountains as they delivered cannon from Fort Prince George to Fort Loudoun. Life had brought many traumatic changes since that time. Fort Loudoun had fallen and most of its officers had been killed, the cannons had been seized and taken to the Cherokee sacred city of Chota, and Joshua and the other surviving Fort Loudoun refugees were imprisoned in various Cherokee towns, facing the possibilities of ransom, a netherworld existence as Cherokee slaves, or death.

The Indian boy's lips moved. His voice was a feverish whisper as he haltingly tried to voice his name. "Tsan . . . Tsanta . . ." He got no further.

That the young Cherokee was sick nearly to the point of death seemed evident to Joshua. Another unwanted surge of pity arose, threatening to bring the tears out of his eyes again. He could not understand his emotions, or what in this situation had aroused them.

Joshua's next action was pure impulse, surprising even himself. Reaching back beneath his loose-fitting shirt, over his head he pulled a deerhide thong that had encircled his neck. On the thong hung an ancient coin with strange words engraved: *Antonius Augustus Pius, Princeps Pontifex Tertio Consule*. Of the words on the other side, only two were legible: *Aurelius Caesar.*

The coin had been one of the few things that Jack Byrum had ever given his son. The trader had obtained the trinket years ago through barter with the recently deceased Cherokee leader Connecorte, whom the whites had called Old Hop. The ancient Indian had told Byrum that the coin had been found, with others like it, beside a river to the west. Byrum had given the coin to his son in a moment of affection, and because such gestures from Byrum were rare indeed, Joshua had guarded the coin closely, finding an inexplicable reassurance and comfort in feeling its cool face lying against his chest. But now he held it up for the Cherokee boy to see, then reached across and placed it in his hands.

"For you," Joshua said in a slightly choked voice. "To help you live." He was amazed at himself as soon as he had done it, amazed he even cared what happened to the sick boy. But care he did.

The Cherokee clutched the coin and breathed loudly, his eyes closing again. Joshua rose, wiped his face again on his sleeve, and turned to go, thinking the Indian was asleep once more. He wondered if the boy, whose mumbled name he had interpreted as Tsani, would ever remember where the coin had come from—if he lived to consider the matter at all.

Joshua had reached the door when the boy made a guttural sound. Looking back, he saw the Indian was trying to give him a gift in return for the coin.

It was the hawk feather, held loosely in his uplifted hand. Joshua knelt again and accepted it. The Cherokee had presented him the only thing he had to give, and to the already emotional Joshua, the gesture was deeply touching.

"I accept your gift," he said, trying to hide his emotions by talking in the haughty style he had heard his father use in bartering with the Cherokees. "And because it is the feather of a hawk, to me you will be Tsani Tlanuwa—John Hawk."

The Indian did not respond. His eyes closed again. For a frightful moment Joshua thought John Hawk had died, but then the troubled breathing started anew.

Joshua rose again and slipped out of the cabin. Outside the door he paused and looked up at the scalplock, and felt ashamed.

Jack Byrum surely would have scorned his son for this failure. The trader had always believed in calculated revenge, believed in it even more strongly, if that was possible, than did the Cherokees he served and also cheated. Joshua had been raised to believe that every blow deserved a responsive one in turn. Today he had been untrue to that belief.

He was sure that what he had done was not right. By rights he should have killed Bloody Eagle's sick nephew instead of giving him a gift and name. No kinsman of Bloody Eagle deserved mercy. Awahili of Tikwalitsi certainly knew nothing of mercy; he was reputed to be a heartless and cruel killer. In the Cherokee towns and even in Fort Loudoun Joshua had heard many tales of the pockmarked warrior's brutality toward the white race that had brought smallpox to the Ani-Yunwiya, as the Cherokees called themselves, leaving him and many others scarred for life. The Fort Loudoun soldiers had even claimed that the bloodred forehead birthmark that had given Bloody Eagle his designation among the whites was the personal mark of the devils he served. Joshua had never been sure what to make of that tale, for he had known many men, his own father included, who seemed faithful enough servants of the devil even without any physical marks to identify them as such.

Somewhere on the other side of Tikwalitsi, the corn mortar was continuing its thumping and grinding. Beyond a line of brilliantly leaved maple trees the Tellico River splashed. Joshua set off across the town again, and as he concentrated on stealth, the October wind snatched the hawk feather from his hand and sent it flying through the air in company with an east-moving shower of golden and crimson leaves. He paused long enough to watch it twist out of sight, then went on.

A NOTE FROM THE AUTHOR

Some years ago a university professor I much admire expressed the opinion that tales of the frontier are to America what the Arthurian legends are to Britain. I agree. The frontier was not only America's proving ground, but also, in large measure, the forge upon which our national identity was hammered out.

Though the frontier as we once knew it is substantially gone, its memories and images remain in our literature, movies, and television, and are thoroughly American in a way little else is. Go almost anywhere on the globe and display a picture of a fur-hatted frontiersman, a trail-dusted cowboy, or a war-bonneted Sioux warrior, and you will find few who do not immediately recognize those images as distinctly and exclusively American.

Early in my typical small-town, 1960s childhood in Cookeville, Tennessee, I became entranced with tales of the American frontier in all their incarnations: books, comics, television, movies. In those years I never knew I would be privileged to someday personally join the tradition of frontier storytelling. The trail was blazed by James Fenimore Cooper and followed, in various ways, by writers as marvelously diverse as Buntline, Grey, Schaefer, L'Amour, Kelton, and McMurtry. I'm glad to have been given the chance, thanks to Bantam Books, to tread my own route as best I can along that well-worn but ever-fresh pathway.

I could not have chosen a more honorable and meritorious literary tradition. Frontier tales, whether traditional westerns or works of historical fiction, are in the last count the signature stories of the American people, for every person on American soil stands at a place that once was the "untamed frontier," or the "Wild West."

I live today in the northeastern portion of Tennessee, in the home county of both Davy Crockett and President Andrew Johnson. My writing, now a full-time career, is expanding to include not only the 19th century West of the vast trans-Mississippi regions, but also my home region in its own frontier period the century before.

Sharing and brightening my life is my wife, Rhonda, who became my bride in 1980 in the shadow of the original gateway to the West, Cumberland Gap, and who remains my greatest supporter and best friend. In the meantime, our three young children, Matthew, Laura, and Bonnie, keep our homefront frontier appropriately wild and woolly.

Cameron Judd
Greene County, Tennessee

ELMER KELTON

☐	27713	**THE MAN WHO RODE MIDNIGHT**	$3.50
☐	25658	**AFTER THE BUGLES**	$2.95
☐	27351	**HORSEHEAD CROSSING**	$2.95
☐	27119	**LLANO RIVER**	$2.95
☐	27218	**MANHUNTERS**	$2.95
☐	27620	**HANGING JUDGE**	$2.95
☐	27467	**WAGONTONGUE**	$2.95
☐	25629	**BOWIE'S MINE**	$2.95
☐	26999	**MASSACRE AT GOLIAD**	$2.95
☐	25651	**EYES OF THE HAWK**	$2.95
☐	26042	**JOE PEPPER**	$2.95
☐	26105	**DARK THICKET**	$2.95
☐	26449	**LONG WAY TO TEXAS**	$2.95
☐	25740	**THE WOLF AND THE BUFFALO**	$3.95

4

4

31

39

39

17

40

21

4
17
21
31
39
40